THE SECRETARY POSITION

PAUL COX

1 – The Jungle

Jane Harris clutched her shoulder bag a little tighter to her body and headed for the subway exit. You couldn't be too careful with these crowds. She always worried that somebody might snatch her bag or her necklace, or the watch on her wrist.

"Sorry," a corpulent dark-haired man with a straw hat on his head yelled in her ear just before he stepped on her foot to get ahead of her.

"It's okay," Jane mumbled, "I walk on them, too."

The escalator up was crowded. And the hot air that blasted her in the face didn't ease the situation. August was not her favorite month anyway. And here, in this subway pit, it was hotter than the mail room of Hades.

She wished she were on her way to some nice air-conditioned office somewhere. Someplace where the coffee wagon carried iced tea, and nobody cared what you did between nine and five. But such was not her fate today.

In feet, she was out of work. Courtesy of her last boss. Mr. George Brook. Vice-President in Charge of Operations of Brook Pen Corporation. Also President of its North American Branch. Jane couldn't imagine that there was a South American branch of Brook. Surely the people in those turbulent countries would have overthrown such an operation long ago. It was a known fact that the Latins revolted against oppressive dictatorships. And Brook Pen Corporation was one, all right.

Jane had grown to loathe it a lot in the three and a half days she had worked there. In fact, she hated it before she started. But she needed the job. God, how she had needed that job! She had been fired, let go, terminated, or laid off every single job since secretarial school two years ago. Something always went wrong. Even when she tried. But this last job was the worst.

She had seen an ad in the paper that said they needed a secretary, an executive secretary. Jane had gone to St. Giles Secretarial School in the city and hadn't done too poorly. At least the male instructors always gave her good grades. But then, they had ever since junior high school. Maybe it had something to do with the fact that she was a sandy blonde stunner with a film star figure and a set of legs to make a racehorse weep with envy. Men had always liked her. And Mr. Brook had, too.

"Yes," the man said, chomping his cigar and swiveling his big cushioned chair to get a better look, "I think we can use a smart girl like you. Of course, the hours are long, the work is tough, and I can't let you make any personal phone calls on my office phones, but the job has its benefits."

Jane was so glad to get the job she didn't even notice that Mr. Brook didn't look at her resume. He was too busy staring at her knees. He also neglected to interview her. Just kept selling her on the job as soon as she sat down and hiked her skirt up a little. The way she had been taught by an instructor at St. Giles.

"Keep that chin up," Mr. Muller would say to her every day after shorthand class. "Keep it up there, young lady. You're learning. That's the important thing. You're trying."

Then he'd follow her out the classroom door, lean toward Jane's blonde hair-covered ear, and whisper, "But if you have any doubts, keep your skirt up, too. Just in case."

Brook never even tested her shorthand. That had been kind of funny. He also never called St. Giles School to see if she had ever been there. He just kept jabbering on about all the "benefits."

And it wasn't long before Jane discovered some of those so-called benefits. One of them was Mr. Brook's inner office.

Jane thought things like that only existed in books. But, sure enough, the first night on the job, after an eight-hour day of busting the copy machine, spilling lighter fluid on the office carpet, and managing to misfile a rather important pencil contract, Jane could hardly believe that the man would actually ask her to stay after hours to do some extra dictation.

Dictation had never been her strong point, really. And Mr. Brook had insisted she write with a company pencil. The damn cheap thing stopped working every time she started to get a flow.

"Sorry," she said, as another word was lost on the pad, "I will try to press harder."

After about ten minutes of trying to get "Dear Sir" down on her steno pad, she was ready to scream.

Brook didn't seem at all disturbed. He laughed a little and swiveled around to face the window. Then, he closed the blinds and stood up.

"I think it's been a very long day for you, Miss Harris," he grinned and hooked his fat firm finger into the vest pocket of his three-piece suit, "I know it has for me. How about some liquid refreshment?"

Jane had been dying for a glass of something cold all day. She managed to miss lunch. She spent the entire hour looking for a pair of cinnamon-colored stockings since one of hers had gotten a runner when she stooped over to file some inane piece of blue paper in some drawer or another.

"How do you like your Scotch?" the big, barrel-chested man asked as he pressed a little button on his desk.

Jane was about to tell him she had never drunk Scotch when she saw the wall on her left split apart and slide off in two opposite directions.

She watched transfixed as the wall receded, and a little room became visible behind it. It was lit in soft, pink lighting, and a stereo's low hum came from within. She saw a little bar come into view where the carpet of the office room now stopped, and beyond it, a fat, enormous white sofa with blue and silver cushions. A little waterfall was set tastefully against the far wall. Tropical plants were sprouting up everywhere. She heard a parrot chattering and saw him fly up and land on a perch over the bar.

"I don't go out much," Mr. Brook said, holding his arm to assist her out of her chair, "so I keep this little home away from home."

Jane could not imagine what Mr. Brook's real home would look like. Tigers in cages, perhaps? Emerald mines? Virgin sacrifice, perhaps. That last thought gave her a little shudder.

"You like?" The man was bending over very close to her.

"Nice," Jane said, putting her steno pad on the floor.

"Why don't you join me inside?" the man said. Somehow, in the interim, he had managed to get to the bar and grab a fifth of liquor. He poured it into glasses when Jane crossed and stepped from the broadloom onto the straw mat.

"You know," the man said in a tired voice, even to him, "I don't share this little room with many people. It's kind of my one big secret."

"I like secrets," Jane managed to say, looking up at the mirrored ceiling. "Sometimes."

"I hope you like mine, Jane," the man said in a voice that sounded insincere, even to him.

At that moment, she heard the office walls slide back into position. She gulped a little sip of the fire liquid in the glass down her throat and wondered if there was any other exit.

"If you want to know something," Mr. Brook said after a few sips. "I think you're just about the nicest thing that's walked into our office since the French cleaning woman flipped out and exposed herself in the reception room."

He let out a hearty bellow and brought his glass down to the bar counter.

"Mr. Brook," Jane began tentatively, "I hope you don't think...."

"Ah, please," he said, draining the last few drops of his drink, "call me George."

"George," was all she got out.

"I'm not wild about that name, but it's my father's. Not wild about my father either, but it's his business."

She waited as he turned morosely toward the mirror behind the bar and poured himself a short second drink.

"Why don't we go over to the sofa and sit a spell?" he said, sounding very friendly and trying not to sound too eager.

"That's fine," Jane said, "provided we lay down a few ground …."

"The girls in the office seem to like you fine," the big man said, lowering himself into the comfort of the waiting cushions.

Now Jane knew he was lying for sure. Three of the girls in the office had walked away when she tried to introduce herself, and one of them had spilled diet soda right into her open purse.

"I can't understand why," she said, trying to sound respectable. "I haven't been working here long enough."

"Long enough," Mr. Brook said, philosophically staring at the ceiling, "how long is long enough?"

Jane fumbled for an answer as he continued.

"I may not have known you long, Jane, but I can tell you something. I like you. Funny how you get a thing about someone. You just know right away whether or not you like them. Know what I'm talking about?"

Jane was afraid she did.

George Brook patted the seat next to him with his big, jeweled hand.

"Come," he said simply, "sit."

Jane made a long, slow cross to his sofa and sat down on the edge as though she were Miss Muffet expecting a spider.

"Come on, girl," the big man bellowed. "Relax. Put your feet up."

"I'll try," she faked gamely.

She kicked off her shoes and felt the straw matting under her stocking feet. She had to admit that the waterfall's wet, running sounds and the parrot's chattering were a nice change from traffic and electric typewriters. But Mr. Brook. Well, he seemed to have something more than dictation on his mind right now. Possibly even something more than a little innocent drinky-poo.

"I want you to be comfortable," he said grandly, gesturing hospitably to the surroundings, "so I'm gonna take off my jacket."

Jane missed his logic, but by the time she thought about it, he had already removed his tie, jacket, vest, and shoes.

"Are you a liberal lady?" the man said, reaching over to open his humidor. He pulled an obscenely huge cigar and ripped off the seal.

"I think I am," Jane said, proud of her Democratic voting record.

"Well," he snorted as he lit his cigar and waved the match out, "you may have a chance to prove that. Why don't you show me your tits."

"What?!" Jane said, her eyes big as soup bowls. "What kind of girl do you think...."

"You already told me you were a liberal lady, remember?"

Jane pulled herself over to one end of the sofa and gripped the big arm in terror. The man had her right where he wanted her, at least in the general vicinity. And he could do almost anything with her. Virgin sacrifice. Ha! That would be just for starters.

George Brook reached out with his enormous paw and hooked one fat, muscular finger around the girl's collar. He dragged her back across the upholstery toward him and grinned down at her.

"From that sweet smile you got," he leered into her face, "I'd say you got all the makings of a good little cocksucker!"

Jane froze under his steel grip as the man reached down with his free hand and yanked his zipper down. It sounded like a wombat just scraped his fingernail along the blackboard. She winced as she saw what he drew out of his crotch basket. It looked like a jackhammer in flesh tights, and she knew it wasn't even fully hard yet.

"Kind of proud of my size," the man said, giving his dick a little shake. Jane dug her fingernails into the sofa seat as she wondered how she would get out of this one.

"I think you'll like it once you get the hang of it." The man said, pulling his huge basketball balls out.

Of course, she might like it, but how would she ever get her mouth around it in the first place?

He moved his hips up and down on the sofa as he brought his tremendous catcher's mitt hand around his thick cock pole. He pulled the foreskin down and swung it in Jane's direction as though he were offering her a refreshment.

"I... I... " Jane was trying to think up something really profound to say to the man, but the slow, hypnotic up-and-down movement of his hand along the thick, hard shaft of his pecker wood disturbed her. She simply couldn't speak.

"I hope you might like to take charge," the man said, gliding his hand slowly over the round smooth knob of his monster prick stick.

Then, he brought it down slowly, all the way to the hilt. The trip took several seconds.

Jane felt her resistance melting away as the man's hard rod grew harder under his slow, rhythmic, pumping hands. She wanted to run, she wanted to puke, she wanted to tell him to fuck himself, but she sat there, frozen. Frozen and watching, The man brought his thick thumb pad to the huge dome of his cock and dabbed at the pre-cum sticking to the slit. He worked a little down over the smooth head and along his shaft. The sounds were sticking to Jane's brain like saltwater taffy. They had also started to stick somewhere else.

She wiggled a little under Brook's still lock-grip hand as she felt herself slowly getting steamier under her silk panties. As if his cock wasn't one of the biggest, fattest, thickest, meanest, longest ones she'd ever seen, those sounds drove her to salivate.

George Brook sat absent-mindedly, staring down at his prick and coaxing it bigger and harder with each stroke. He knew it wouldn't be long before this little girl would give in and suck him. She had to. She couldn't possibly resist the lure of his hot throbbing rod. No woman had yet. He worked his hand a little faster up and down the shaft and felt the veins beneath his grip coming to the surface.

"Could I?" Jane heard herself say. She sounded like a wind-up doll in a nursery.

"Here," the man said, smiling grotesquely and bringing

her tiny hand to rest on the head of his wide, hard schlong. "Knock yourself out."

He reached down to the ashtray for his cigar. He loved to puff on that thing while somebody beat his meat. Preferably somebody young, petite, blonde, and not too bright. Jane Harris was to the manner born.

Jane recoiled at the firm yet spongy touch of the man's prick knob. It was slightly tacky and vibrated when she made contact with it.

"Go on," the big man said, feeling very content with himself, "touch away."

Jane tried to bring her whole hand around his shaft, but it wouldn't reach. Then she assisted herself with her other hand and encircled his giant, man meat by reaching her thumb and index finger around it.

"Fast thinking," George said, bringing his feet to rest on the coffee table and feeling his prick harden up a little.

Jane bit her lower lip and drew her gliding fingers down the man's long cock pole. The grease from his slit eased her along until she got to the hilt. She felt his hard, steely balls under the palms of her hand and couldn't decide whether or not it would be appropriate to play around with them. They seemed so lewdly inviting.

"Just keep that up a little," the man moaned, confident in his ability to last at least another eight seconds as the little nymphet glanced over his glans with her two spread hands and her tongue hanging out.

Jane began to instinctively pump her hands up and down the wet, slapping hard member and felt it grow still more rigid under the skin of her hands. The action was arousing her to a fever pitch. She bit down on the tongue hanging out between her lips and cried out a little pain.

"Getting to you?" the big man said, laughing a little and exhaling a massive puff of Havana smoke.

Jane wanted to deny it, but she didn't think it would be convincing, especially since she had already started to drool onto her chin, and her left knee was shaking like a maraca against her right one.

"Why don't you try giving it a little suck?" he said, trying to fight the uncontrollable urge to let out a whoop every time the girl's fingers met atop his prick knob. She had begun to pick a nice rhythm, all right. Maybe she would prove to be a good cocksucker.

"I don't know," Jane tried as she felt Mr. Brook's enormous paw strike her down to within an inch of his vibrating ramrod.

She swallowed hard and looked into his hot, wet cock slit. She felt herself soften in the core, and her panties grew more moist with every breath she took. She was starting to feel hot and bothered. Steamy and torrid. The tropical surroundings were getting to her. And they were getting to her right between her legs.

"Oh," she said as she felt the man's hand close around her left tit.

George could feel the tight air-born mass of perfectly circular flesh beneath his huge hand. He wanted to feel more. He reached down and massaged her right tit hard under his hand. Then he found the buttons on her blouse and twisted them out of their holes one by one. His cock wracked and flailed hard the whole time.

Jane felt her blouse slide off her shoulders and the man's hand reach for her bra hook. It didn't take long for him to disengage the hook and eye, and she just stared into the eye of the big prick the whole time.

"Big succulent tits," Brook mumbled. "My favorite kind."

He fingered the girl's smooth, rubbery nipples in between his fingers as he brought her head down on his cock. He could feel the hot breath of her mouth steaming it up just before he felt the wet tongue press hard against the shiny, round dome.

Jane glided her tongue around the rim of the man's big thick wet crown and flicked it across his shaft a few times. It tasted delicious. Good enough to eat. She couldn't help herself any longer. It was just too much for her. She couldn't hold back. That seemed to be the law of the jungle. And she was set right down in the middle of one right now. The incessant chattering of the parrot, the rush of the little waterfall, the stereo music all told her that.

She felt overwhelmed by a surging desire to suck the man's cock. Her thighs ached with passion, and her cunt flowed with the juice of excitement.

She popped the man's big prick into her mouth and began sucking on it hard. She slid her head down to the hilt and rolled her tongue around the wet, pulsating log as she worked her mouth back up, slowly, slowly, and teasingly. She coiled her head around and sucked the man clockwise, then reversed it and sucked him counterclockwise. All the time, she kept her up-and-down movements slow and rhythmic. She went up again and vibrated her hot, eager tongue around the head before she slid back down his shaft and sucked him hard at the base of his peter. His balls felt like a rock garden under a flagpole.

"You do that well, kid," the big man said, smiling at the mirrors above. He was getting a superb bird's eye view of what the girl was doing to him. As she came off a moment, he could see his huge, long prick pole glistening in the dim light of the room. Then she disappeared over it again, sucking and flicking her tongue all the way down.

"Do that, Kid!" he heard himself say, kneading her tits between his fingers and thrusting his hips up high to receive her eager mouth hole. She had him in such a tight lock he could feel the friction mounting to a white heat.

"Oh, shit, do that, do that to me. God, that's it. Don't stop. Suck me. Christ, suck me. Do it. Oh, God, suck the shit out of me. Suck that pecker. Suck that big prick."

Jane was sliding up and down as hard as a piston in high gear. She let the saliva roll out of her hot, horny mouth as she dove down hard and came up easy on the man's enormous fuck stick. She hit him again and again, like waves of pleasure, like non-stop washes of agonizing desire. She hit his cock again and again with her sucking, spinning mouth.

"Fuck!" the man called out, pinching her tits together and pulling hard on the big thumb nipples. "I'm gonna shoot!"

He thrust his hips up high and hard into her mouth. Then he split his cock slit open with the force of his shooting spunk. It came bursting out of his prick hole, right out the end of his pecker. It came spurting out uncontrollably in white, hot rushes of thick, comey goo.

Jane bolted her head up on its impact. The hot, wet spunk stuff hit her so hard it rocked her head back a moment. Then she felt the rush, the delicious pouring rush of white, hot cream. She felt the spurting buckets full of heavy, hot jism spewing all over the back of her throat. It aimed at every pore, every flesh pocket of her insanely tight little mouth gripper. She buckled right down on it. She came back down it hard and eagerly lapped it up. She licked and sucked and slurped and swallowed every ounce of the thick come cream. She ate the hot white liquid as eagerly and happily as a puppy drank milk.

"Fucking little Sucker!" the man yelled, surprised to find that the girl actually had performed so admirably under fire. Jane ate some man spunk off her lips and then licked the corners to make sure she had gotten it all. Then she sat up.

The man stared at her high round titties as they bounced into place when she straightened her back. They were every bit as stunning as they had felt delectable. He could feel his numb, still rock-hard pecker begin to nod.

Pity, he thought, he would have liked to have fucked the little Cocksucker right then and there.

"Is it hot in here?" Jane said, looking over at the waterfall.

Mr. Brook shook his prick and folded it back into his pants. "I think you're a little hot." He said, zipping his pants up. "No, I think you're quite a hot little number. That's what I think. Like another drink?"

Jane reached out and shoved the metal frame of the revolving door as hard as she could. She just couldn't believe how Mr. Brook had changed. He seemed so nice that first day, if a little forward. But still, two and a half days later, he fired her like all the others.

What had she done? What had been her crime? All right, so she was no great shakes as a secretary. But Mr. Brook said she gave great head. He never stopped raving about it, in fact.

The next day had been a little more fun. Not until after work, but she was on a heavy overtime schedule. He had invited her into his office again, same scenery. Then the wall opened up, and they strolled into the jungle. This time, he insisted on going down on her. It was fun. In fact, her pussy smarted a little just thinking about it as she pushed the elevator button of the colossal stone skyscraper she was standing in.

The elevator finally did come, and the door split open. Jane half-expected to see a little jungle setting with a bar in one corner, but no luck. She scrambled in just as the doors started to close again. Then, forty people rushed in after her, holding the door open for each other as they did so. Then, the elevator sat there for another minute and a half, so packed you couldn't get a notepad inside. Finally, the doors thudded shut, and things headed skyward.

Jane took in her breath and let it all out. She was practicing relaxing. She needed to relax. She had to look calm. Calm and lovely. Serene. Even though it was ninety-five degrees outside, the peak of lunch hour, and she was ready to scream from desperation. She felt desperate. She tried not to feel desperate. All right, so she needed a job. All right, so she had no references worthy of the name. She hadn't worked more than three and a half days in any one place in two years. These things happened, right?

"Getting out," she said from the corner as the elevator touched down on the tenth floor.

She wiggled her sensuous hips through the crowd and stepped out. She hoped the place would be sensible. Reasonable. She hoped to hell they would give her a job at least.

"Won't you please have a seat, Miss Harris?" the receptionist invited. She gestured to the plastic row of orange seats in the waiting area.

Jane noticed about fifteen other people were ahead of her. She was going to have a long wait. Too bad she hadn't brought something to read. She sat back and looked at the plastic ferns growing out of the corners.

Mr. Brook had really turned into one sour lemon, all right. And that second evening had been such fun! He even gave her a little gift. A tiny gold heart on the end of a chain. Then they had another drink, and he fucked her under the waterfall.

Wild and wet. That would describe it best. Very wet. He had coaxed her under that waterfall. Promised her a really good time. And he had been good.

"What are you doing on that coffee table? Don't you know staying dry is not where it's at, Jane?" George said, peeling his shirt over his shoulders and ripping it off his wrists.

He was standing on the little rock wall that banked against the pool where the waterfall fell. He already had his pants off, and that monster schlong of his was dangling about halfway down to his knees.

"I don't know," she said, trying hard to resist the lure of the wild, rollicking falls as they hit the asphalt rocks strewn in its path and coursed over the plants growing out from the wall. "I can't swim."

"Not to worry, Doll," the big man bragged, sticking his toe in the water. "I was a junior lifeguard in college. I'll save you should anything go wrong."

And he had. Once he got her into the water, ripped her dress off, and rubbed his hard hands all over her body, she slipped and fell. He had to pull her up by that sandy blonde hair and wipe it out of her eyes. Then, of course, he shoved her up against the rock wall and plugged the daylights out of her tight little cunt.

Jane could still remember how Mr. Brook looked at her when she had her clothes off.

"That's a classy little cunt you got there," he smiled, pulling her pussy lips back and admiring the view. She was rosy hot pink, and wet inside. It looked like the perfect place to park his long cock. Jane blanched fascia as the man explored her pussy locale. She loved how his thick, tough fingers felt as they parted her tingling plump cunt lips.

"Oooooh," she said, feeling the ecstasy rush to the spot and supply more blood to her throbbing cunt veins as the man brought his thick, sensual lips down to her pussy and pressed them around the rim of her hole.

Then the man took his semi-hard man meat in his hands and ran it around the whole perimeter of her pussy inner lip ridges. The contact points made her gasp with excitement.

He brought his full thick cock head in between her lips

and made for her wet, quivering hole. He stuck the huge knob inside and worked it hard until her cunt juices and pre-cum fluid mixed enough to allow him the necessary lubrication to forge ahead.

”That hurts,” the girl shouted as he worked his stiff cock wand into the pink grip lock. He had to work the head very hard back and forth, back and forth, to make any headway. Penetration of this tight little chick was not as easy as she looked willing to be.

”Ouch!” she said as he stuck himself in a little higher, still backtracking every little bit to ease the way in with joy juices from the both of them.

Jane felt the man’s full sail masthead heave to and fro inside her tight pink twat. It burned, stung, and ached like fury, but she didn’t tell him no. It felt like he was trying to get two cars into a single garage, but she never once protested. She thought for a few seconds that from the size of the man’s loaf and the size of her wee box cunt that he was going to cut off her air. To choke her. Then, she remembered that she didn’t breathe from her twat.

”God, this feels like a fuck fest to me,” the man shouted as he plunged his giant wick into her tiny jam jar. He wanted to just take ahold of her slim, frail shoulders and slam on into home, but he thought better of it. Chicks like her needed to be primed before they could be adequately pumped. That’s what he intended to do.

He reached around and grabbed her clit between his thumb and his index finger. He shook a few jerks hard and felt it rise like a leech full of blood. He massaged it hard, then harder between his fingers as he continued to ram his big fuck stick into her swollen, raw pussy hole.

"Oh, my God," Jane moaned, "I can't take much more of that."

"Too bad," George said, plugging her a little more, "I got a lot more to give you. Just hang on, Honey."

He slid still more of his thick meat rack into her tight, hot fuck pipe. The wrapping, packing, gripping, slipping motion was unbearably sweet.

Then he sunk his rod into her hole up to his hilt and held it there for an interminably long time. He circled it a bit, in opposition to the circles he was making with his finger on her engorged love button. Then her cries came into his ears again.

"God, it's too much; it's just fucking too much." She moaned.

He saw that her face had turned red, and her eyes rolled back into her head. So he started pumping her harder. He pumped her like a drill as if she was an untried oil bed. He plugged the stuffing out of her as he pulled his rod almost out and pushed it back in again.

He brought his free hand around the front and massaged her high, fleshy tit cups.

Jane looked down and saw the man's thick bronzed-tone arm against the soft white of her ice cream mound tits. She saw him grasp the nipple of one of her eager hot tits in his fingers and squeeze it hard. Then she felt it. She felt it through her tit, back to her rib cage, and down to her toes. Then it ricocheted back up and hit her at the base of her brain.

"Owww," she screamed loud enough to scare the parrot.

"Am I hurting you, Sugar?" the man said between gasps for air.

"Noooo," Jane wailed back to him. "I'm coming....."

George wracked his meat wildly against the girl's womb opening and squeezed his butt muscles together hard as he fondled her breasts and diddled her thick clit button with a vengeance. He felt he might break the little thing in two. Slam, bang, slam, bang. He was rocking his rock-hard pecker in and out. Out and in. No slowing down now. No easing up or showing off. No way. He felt his cock gear go in for the big grip, and he tensed every muscle.

Then he felt his balls cram up inside themselves and flick a trigger deep inside his bowels. Then he heard something go BANG!

He blew his spunk load out the end of his cannon. He exploded the gun barrel of his cock, and a high-powered load of cock come came out of it. He banged, and he fired his semen weapon all up inside the wiggly, wet, squirm hole of the girl's cunt. His cock shot, and the cunt took it. That was right on target.

Jane felt herself pull up into a spasm of non-stop orgasms. She was coming and coming and coming. A string of firecrackers went off inside her, one after the other. Pop, pop, pop. She twisted and jerked her whole body with each wild orgasm. Every come was more intense than the previous. She couldn't find the brakes. The man's big huge dick kept firing, and she kept repeating the gunshots. She spilled her juice. She oozed the come stuff out her crevice and down on George's finger. She let go of her juice load down her leg and along

George's thick, veined cock pole. It ran down his pecker; it ran into rivulets down his balls. It covered his pecker and his balls and flowed down his thigh.

"I think you just shot your stuff, Little Lady," he said as he watched his milky liquid follow hers down both legs and head for the bubbling water.

"God, that hurt," the girl sobbed as she ran one hand through her still-soaking sandy locks of hair. She wondered how she would be able to sit down the next day at her desk. Her pussy was throbbing with pain so hot and hard, her ass was numb.

But the next day, she did find her chair. And she sat in it. Until five o'clock. Then Mr. Brook asked her to come into his office for more "dictation."

"Are you reading that?" a cute young man said, leaning over her and pointing to the open magazine she had spread across her lap.

She must not have been fooling him by letting it lie there. And the truth was, she wasn't reading it. She gave it to him and smiled wanly.

"Miss Harris," the receptionist's coolly efficient voice wafted toward her. "You're next."

Indeed she was. She could see from the waiting room's appearance that not much movement had occurred since she sat down. But sure enough, as luck would have it, she was next.

"There's an excellent ad on page twelve," she said to the cute guy, "other than that, the magazine's a total waste."

She held onto the strap of her shoulder bag and disappeared into a little cubicle.

A broad-shouldered middle age man sat behind the desk. He was wearing a dark tan suit and a big, flashing grin. He seemed to like what Jane had shown him in that first moment.

"Miss Harris," he said, standing up and extending a massive, solid hand with sturdy, elongated fingers. "Bobby Dune."

"Hello," she said, sitting down. She was so intent on looking at the rugged hunk behind the desk that she forgot to swing her shoulder bag onto her lap and promptly sat on it. She rose swiftly off her seat and swung the damned thing up where it belonged.

"How's the weather out there?" The hunk said, reaching up and scratching his ear. Jane wondered if it would split his seam. His muscles were bulging that hard.

"Beastly," Jane replied, smiling coyly. She hoped to hell he hadn't seen her resume.

"I've just been looking over your resume," he said, shaking his head. "Frankly, Miss Harris, your work record is less than superlative."

"I know," she said, casting her eyes toward the linoleum. "Life hasn't been too kind these past two years."

"I hope you'll understand that we might have difficulty placing you in a good job, given your work record."

"I didn't come to this agency for a good job."

"What did you come for? This is a job agency."

"I came for a job. Any job!"

"Hmmmmm," the man said, stroking his chin and leaning on one elbow. "Stand up again."

Jane stood up and brought her weight to one foot. She

licked her lips to check for lip gloss and stared back at Mr. Dune.

”Would you wait here one moment?” he said, standing up. He looked like a linebacker for a pro football team.

She nodded her head as he strolled through the half-glass door. He did not return till after she had scraped all the fingernail polish off her fingers.

”I think I may have a line for you.” He was really grinning now. So hard that Jane saw that one of his teeth was solid gold.

”I’ve heard a few this week,” she said, trying to sound hopeful but sadly fearing she missed the mark. ”What is it?”

”Ever hear of the firm Temporary Secretary? ” he said, busily writing some information onto a white card.

”No,” she said, shaking her head. ”I thought I’d heard of all the temporary worker agencies. I’ve worked for most of them, uh, temporarily.”

”I’m not surprised,” the man replied, scribbling away furiously with a thick ballpoint pen. ”They’re a small outfit. And, I better add, exclusive. They specialize in hard-to-place candidates.”

”Well, that’s me,” Jane replied, remembering to cross her legs and hike up her skirt. It was a little late, but it never hurt to take out insurance.

”They’re located not far from here.” He finished his scratching and handed her a card with an address on it. And a name. Jane could barely make it out.

”I can walk here?” Jane said, still trying to figure out her way around the big city.

”Oh, yes,” he said, standing up and extending his hand toward hers. ”It has been a pleasure, I assure you.”

”Thank you so much,” Jane said, finding herself in a curtsey pose as she clutched her card between her fingers and felt strangely optimistic.

”I shall leave you on a precautionary note, Miss Harris,” the athletic hunk said, ”Temporary Secretary works with some of the top clients in the city. And in the world. But they may appear a little peculiar at first.”

”Oh?” she said, blinking her eyes like headlights in the fog.

”They have some unusual ways of screening new candidates.”

Jane cocked her head to one side and looked into the man's tanned good-looking face. Nothing she hadn't probably already been through. Considering how Mr. Brook had already screened her without her knowing in advance that it would be peculiar, this place sounded refreshing.

”Bye,” the tall hulk said as he opened the door for her.

She could smell the distinctively woodsy smell of his cologne as she sailed off through the open door and out.

2 – The Tests

Willowy, raven-haired Vicky West put the telephone receiver back into its cradle and stared out the window of the mammoth skyscraper. So Temporary Secretary, Inc. was to have a brand new applicant. She pulled a pencil out of her desk. Bobby only sent a few applicants her way. Only those with that unique quality. Only those who didn't make it as secretaries by the usual standard. But then, hers was not the usual standard. Temporary Secretary was not the typical temporary job agency.

She swung her legs out from under the desk and glanced at the tiny hole in her black silk stockings. It was small now, but those things had a way of stretching out into ragged holes big enough to stick a fist into. She worked the high gloss fingernail of her right hand into it and pulled it away from her leg. It was a hole, all right. She would have to change those stockings before that new one, what was her name, "Miss Harris," got here.

Vicky stepped to the supply closet and pulled it open by the handle. It folded in fourths, and she reached for the light. Then she stood back to look. Red mesh, blue mesh, silver mesh, fishnet, velour, nylon, every damn color size and description of stocking hanging there and not a single one in black silk. She would just have to go out and get some. Later.

Then she eyed the rest of the clothing on the racks. Full-length black satin and leather corsets. Iron-maiden waist cinchers. Leather boots with stiletto heels. Many leather bras and camisoles of various styles and descriptions.

Vicky was proud of her wardrobe, all right. It had taken a long time to accumulate it. Much of the leather and metal gear had to be specially ordered. But it was worth it, every penny of it.

She grabbed a pair of black nylon stockings with rosette seams and kicked off her high-heeled shoes. Then she opened the closet door wider and gazed in the mirror. She had a body on her, all right. Stacked, as they say. And she was proud of it. She dressed it in the finest satin, lace, and leather that money could buy. She had earned it.

Temporary Secretary, Inc. was her baby, after all. She had pioneered it. And it had paid handsomely for those who played along. Tired executives after bored vice presidents, even presidents had benefited from Temporary Secretary's unique customer service. They had learned discipline at some of the hands of the city's finest mistresses of pain and pleasure.

"Hello, Temporary Secretary," she had heard countless chief executive officers say over the telephone. "Could you send me one of your finest secretaries? I need a girl who can handle a particularly tough situation."

Of course, Vicky had sent over a young dominatrix who knew how to make those men behave.

How many private office suites had been turned into dens of discipline because she ran this kind of operation? How many thankful, appreciative executives were still smarting from the lessons they had received at the hands of her employees?

And it had started out so simply. Only ten months ago.

She had been working at a job agency just down the street, she had met Bobby Dune there, and it had been okay, as far as those things go.

She was a strikingly tall and shapely young woman who never had trouble handling people – never had all her life. And she liked handling them. She liked to get as much domination over them as she could, as often as she could, as a matter of fact.

"I'm looking for an extraordinary girl," an aged, shaking voice had come to her over the telephone one day, "I do hope you understand."

Vicky hadn't. Not at that moment, anyway. But she found out in a hurry.

"My name is Carl Winter. I am the president of Winter's Woodware. I assure you my credentials are unquestionable. Check me up if you like. I only recently lost my best secretary. She got married and moved out of town. I am so terribly afraid to call any of these sleazy houses of ill-repute."

At that statement, Vicky blanched. What the hell was this old codger after? Still, something about his voice, his position, and his money made her listen on.

"I don't take my discipline lightly. Oh, dear, I hope I'm not coming on too strong. Please let me assure you price is no object. No object whatsoever. Do we understand each other?"

Vicky nodded her head in silence. The man on the other end of the phone blotted his sweating forehead with his handkerchief and hung on. It was a long shot, all right. One that might not work, but he had to give it a try. He was desperate. And he was afraid to call one of those places that ran ads in the newspaper for such things. He didn't trust anyone not listed with the Chamber of Commerce.

The black-haired beauty pondered a moment. Then she relaxed and spoke easily into the phone."I think perhaps we can help you, Mr. Winter. But, of course, I would personally have to set an appointment with you, check out the surroundings, and set a fee. You see, I couldn't send just any girl on such a sensitive and special assignment."

"Oh, no, no, no," the man replied,"I wouldn't want you to. By all means, come. I welcome the opportunity to meet you. I'm certain that if we can come to some kind of arrangement, I can help you in the future."

Vicky hung up the phone and checked herself in the mirror. She was in her tweedy conservative stage then, though her figure was not conservative. It was lushly, roundly, fully, hotly developed, with curves aiming out and up and around and over. She thought she looked safe enough to fool anyone and patted her huge black twist knot on top of her head. That was tame enough looking to fool anybody.

Mr. Winter's office was well-appointed. Carpets you could sink into, Italian Renaissance furniture. Nothing but the best. And Mr. Winter was nothing to sneeze at either.

From their phone conversation, she gathered he was aged. He sounded so shaky, probably from fright. He was a sizable man. Broad-shouldered and silver-haired. Handsome, well-muscled, and rich. Very, very rich.

"Won't you come right in, Miss West?" he said, shocking the receptionist who had asked her to sit and wait her turn. Everybody wanted to see Mr. Winter.

She entered a posh, sparsely furnished inner office with a spectacular view of the city and several admirably good works of art on the walls.

"Have a seat, my dear," he said, guiding her to a high-back white upholstered chair. "I do hope we can speak frankly," he said, leaning back against his enormous desk, "I am a man who likes to come right out and say what's on my mind. At my age, I haven't time to play games."

"I appreciate that," Vicky said in the most aggressive voice she could manage. She may have been new to whatever Mr. Winter proposed, but something told her to keep her chin out. And keep her skirt up.

"Won't you step this way? I've something to show you. My dear secretary left these things here. I'm determined to keep them for her …. uh, until she comes for them, of course."

"Of course," Vicky said, flashing her deep amber eyes and rising from her seat.

The two made for another inner office, and Mr. Winter flicked on the lights. The place was well-furnished and tasteful, like all the other rooms she had seen. An enormous boardroom table filled this one. Giant, soft, blue cushioned chairs surrounded it.

A board room, Vicky thought, nothing too unusual here, so far.

As she glanced around, Mr. Winter had opened a closet and stuck his head in. He pulled out a suitcase and brought it down with a soft thud onto the boardroom table top.

"These have such sentimental value," the man said as he

flicked the clasp on the suitcase and pulled it open. "I do hope they'll come to mean as much to you as they do to me."

Vicky had no idea what the man had in store here. But she had been around many demanding men, many eccentric men, some even downright kinky. And she had been able to cater to each and every one of them. The only requirement, she had found, was an open mind. An open mind and little willingness. The desire for big bucks didn't hurt either.

"I have such a fondness for Florentine leather," the old man said, pulling out a full-length jumpsuit with a heavy industrial metal zipper and a very plunging neckline. The entire piece was studded with silver studs from shoulder to cuff. "I collect fine things. And this one, I'm especially proud of."

He withdrew a long, single strand of leather thong and tugged a bit to free the other end from under the pile of goodies.

Vicky tried not to flinch as a stout leather handle emerged. She knew, by then, that Mr. Winter was holding a whip. A long, black leather one.

He reached into the suitcase again and pulled out a pair of high-heel leather boots and a long cord, some handcuffs, chains, and two C-clamps.

"Can you help me," he said plaintively to Vicky, "I'm in terrible need, and I've been such a bad boy."

He shook his head and cast his eyes down toward the carpet. He reached for a handful of the dominance equipment and shoved it across the top of the table to where she stood.

Vicky took a long, hard look at the stuff. It would be a challenge, no doubt. And, being as how Mr. Winter was an important client, she figured it best to come out square with him. "I see no reason why we can't come to terms, Mr. Winter," she said forcefully. "I want you to know, however, right from the start, that I am a little …. how shall I say it …. new to this sort of business venture."

"Not to worry, Miss West," he said, in a grandfatherly tone as he stroked the leather whip lovingly with his firm, sturdy fingers, "I'll be here, too. Nothing to worry about. And I think I can tell, from the way you carry yourself, that you'll be quite suitable to the task."

He smiled a devilishly little boy smile and brushed his hand over the black and silver pile of equipment.

"May I change somewhere?" Vicky said, feeling that she was quite ready to try anything after his reassuring words.

"Ah, yes," the man said, indicating a little room off to one side, "there's a bathroom right here. Ah, you'll need a mask, too, I believe. Such lovely hair," he said, rubbing his hands together gently.

Vicky disappeared into the bathroom and took her dominance equipment with her. She slipped out of her clothes quickly and turned to the mirror. God, she loved looking at herself in the mirror, any mirror. And this was going to be fun. There was a full-length one right on the back of Mr. Winter's executive bathroom door.

She unsnapped her pink satin bra and pulled it over her tremendous air-born tits. They sparkled and shone out creamy ivory in the diffused light of the bathroom. Her nipples were dark circles of bumpy, reptile hide. They were the size of silver dollars and stood out so far that it looked like they had been fitted onto her enormous breasts.

She slipped her pink nylon panties down over her tight, curvy hips and slid them over her thighs. Her shiny black bush looked lustrous and inviting as it reflected in the mirror. Through it, she could barely make out her huge, thick pink cunt lips.

She left her own black garter belt on and unhooked her rather conservative beige stockings, and replaced them with a thick, tight pair of black mesh ones.

Then she dug into the pile and pulled out a severe half-bra with wires and stays. She put it on and shook her big tits into it by bending over toward the front as she hooked it in the back. Then she looked at herself.

The effect was dramatic. Her tits rose straight up toward the roof in that thing, and the tops of her nipple circles were quite visible. She became aroused almost immediately as she took in this picture of herself. Her black hair made a perfect match to the theatrically black undergarments.

Then she found the leather jumpsuit and put it on. It fit her like a shrunk glove. When she zipped up the metal zipper, which started under her legs, she noticed how it pressed her tits firmly together in a forced cleavage fashion. She let the zipper down so that her tits bounced a little down into the opening. Still, they stuck together so hard it looked like they had been glued.

The boots came on after. They were so tight they weren't easy to get into. They added nearly another six inches to her already above-average height. They were of finest black leather with a thick, wood and metal sole. The heel was a single blade of deadly-looking stiletto. She was sure she could have put somebody's eye out with it.

She took in the whole picture and felt immensely satisfied with herself. She looked the part, the part she had seen displayed in movies and magazines but never had the opportunity to try. Now, at long last, was her opportunity, the perfect opportunity.

She opened the door and strode importantly to the table. Mr. Winter was sitting in the corner with his eyes downcast. He wore absolutely nothing except a thick, french-cut leather jock strap. His body was in excellent form. His muscles were well-toned and enormous.

"All right," she said, just the way she did when she was an office manager at her last job, "Let's get to work."

Vicky remembered that incident quite well. She loved going over it now and again. It was good to be reminded of what had happened that day. And it had been less than a year ago. Mr. Winter had become her first client. Their session together had been immensely successful. He had even encouraged her to start the business she now ran. Had helped her financially. He had been impressed with her gifts as a dominatrix.

She smiled and closed the door of the closet. Then she returned to her desk and turned on the stereo. Some soothing music. That would make the young lady feel at home.

Mr. Winter had been so cooperative that first day. And he had never let her down since. Two and three times a week, he called for a "special girl" to come and relieve his boring routine.

Mostly, he asked for Vicky but was content with whomever she sent him. She trained the girls personally, so she knew they would be up to par. Executives expected the best. And Mr. Winter got the best. He said so himself. That first day.

"You'll need these, Mistress," he said, helpfully holding a pair of handcuffs. He also gave her some shackles that she used to bind his feet to the legs of the boardroom table.

"Lie silent," she told him, finding her most authoritative voice to speak in.

He had obeyed willingly as she gagged his mouth with a black band and worked feverishly to cuff his wrists and tie the metal cuffs together under the table. She thought she had him pretty tied up and bound by the time she started for the whip.

That was one thing she was a little hesitant about. She had never whipped anyone, though she had slapped some girls around who couldn't seem to behave themselves in the office. Office managers had to be tough. But no whips; the boss wouldn't have allowed it.

However, it simply did not prove to be too difficult. She thought she had the hang of it quite decently, in fact. She simply brought the thing up over her head, cracked it, and brought it down on Mr. Winter's high spread-eagle ass cheeks.

How he had screamed in pain! "Aaaaahhhhhhhhhhh," he protested as she reared her arm up and again brought the leathery rein down to meet his quivering butt mounds.

"Oh, Mistress," the man said, "what did I do to deserve this?"

"You slimy, disgusting piece of office furniture," she shouted, flailing that thing down hard again and actually reddening his ass this time, "you don't deserve to draw another breath."

Then she belted him again. By now, she was noticing red welt trails where she had lashed him severely. But he seemed to be responding well to this harsh treatment. And he took his punishment like a man, too. She had to admit. She also had to admit something else. She was starting to like doing this. It seemed the natural order of things, really.

Here was a man, completely helpless, bound and gagged and lying flat against the table, with his ass raised up to receive her cruel whip blows. She was in complete control, total power. What could be more fitting? She, the temptress of time immemorial, and he was her willing subservient. After all, didn't she know best? She had always thought she did.

"Eat my whip!" she shouted and broke the still again with a piercing snap of leather as she brought the whirling thing down on his helpless backside.

Carl Winter shrank into the glossed table top and withered with ecstasy. He loved to break in a new young dominatrix. Especially one with this much natural inclination. She was regal and haughty and extremely beautiful. All the requirements necessary to make a full-fledged Class A mistress. And he had become her total slave. It hadn't taken her long to swing into high gear either. He winced as he felt the bite of the whip savagely slash his buttocks.

After five minutes of intermittent lashings, the man had become so imbued with pleasure and heightened sensations of lust he begged to be let off the table.

Finally, when she was good and ready, she let him. She

made him get down on all fours and rode him around like a trick pony. She beat his butt with an English-riding crop and dug her boots into his stomach flesh as she pranced around the floor with him under her.

She had even adjusted a little harness, made specially to fit him, around his head and over his mouth, and reined him in any direction she wanted him to go.

"Move, you lowly scum spot," she bellowed, kicking his ribs with her boot heel and forcing him to carry her this way and that, faster and faster.

Finally, after riding him hard, she let down the thick gold zipper in his kid skin jock strap and eased his schlong out with one leather-gloved fist.

Then she beat his backside to a pulp as she forced him to jerk himself off in front of her. His face was a mass of weathered wrinkles and etched with pain. He begged her; he pleaded with her to let him go, to stop this insane charade once the gag was out of his mouth. But she whipped him so forcefully, so harshly, he finally controlled his tongue and bent to her wishes.

She let him kiss her boottips as he jerked himself off with one hand. He had a long firm cock handle, too, and a steady gliding hand to serve it. The better to service her, she thought.

He whacked himself however she commanded. Slower, faster, harder, softer, whatever her pleasure was, as she sat in one of the huge chairs with her feet up, displaying her open wet cunt to his face. She wouldn't let him close, though. She forced him to continue jerking himself as she played with a long five-lash leather whip along his flanks and down into his ass crevice.

From where she sat, she could see him perfectly articulating his massive cock up and down under his hand. She made him pull his balls out of the tiny zipper and saw him squint in pain as he did so. They must have pinched him terribly in that position. Then she made him masturbate at her feet, kissing her boot and licking him with the whip the entire time.

Carl Winter felt his balls pinched so hard; he knew they must have turned blue, but it was worth it. The excruciatingly delicious rush he was getting from this woman was worth anything. She was the complete mistress. His dream dominatrix.

He gobbled eagerly at her boot tip. He licked the sole of her shoe, demeaning position. So low, so brutally, unthinkably beneath contempt. And here he was, down on the floor, crawling in filth and debasement and loving every putrid second.

"Lick, you despicably unworthy worm!" the woman said, sounding like the Red Queen ordering Alice's head off.

Mr. Winter was whacking his hot, wet pickle as hard as she would allow him now, and he felt very, very close to shooting his juice. But the long, slow build-up to this moment had filled him with such longings and desires he hoped he could hold out a little more.

"Not until I tell you," she commanded, bringing her free boot up to his cock and pressing every so firmly on his already-aching balls.

”Mistress,” he wailed, ”please, I'll do anything, anything to please you.”

”You'll come when I say and not before,” the woman spat at him.

Vicky was feeling herself getting so hot by this time she had to pick up that English riding crop and fiddle herself with the stout handle of it. She rubbed that hard leather core against her clit and felt it rise with the full pressure of engorged blood. It smacked and whomped against the leather thickness and pulsated and hissed against her cunt lips. The heightening of her own pleasure on her own time gave her a power rush almost as fine as the one she was getting from dominating Mr. Winter.

”Oooohhh,” she said, trying to control her volume. The sight of that man down on his knees, slurping on her leather boots, jacking himself like a pile driver, the feelings of arousal under her own hand as she stroked and massaged her hot hard clit with the leather crop, all these feelings added up to one giant tower of desire.

The man grabbed his pecker wood harder and dug his fist as the woman commanded. He beat it more savagely, waiting for her orders. He hoped they wouldn't be long coming. The pressure under his cock head, along his glistening hot shaft, down to the base of his prick pole, was mounting like a tidal wave.

”Now,” the woman shouted.

Carl stuck his tongue back in his mouth and concentrated solely on plunging his big ringer hand down and up the full length of his wicked, willing cock stick. He plugged himself harder, harder with his whacking, wet hand. He fixed his gaze down onto his mistress's huge black boot, struck his hot hand wad tight against his cock, and worked it ever faster all the way up and down, down and up his slick wet shaft.

"Aaaahhh," he said as he let out a huge load of spunk from the top of his flagellating pecker. "Eiieeeeeeeee," he shouted as he shot his spunk bank up and onto his mistress's shiny black boot toe. He shot more of it up as high as the rim of her black boot and a little onto the soft leather of her jumpsuit leg. His spunk seemed interminable. His juice wouldn't stop. His bucket overflowed and sprang in every direction. His cup was running over.

"Come you, Sucker!" Vicky cried as she slashed her slave with the teasing leather thongs of the five-piece whip. She lashed him harder, watching him shoot his white load over her boot.

Then she felt her hold on herself give way as the excitement of arousal touched her insides in a place she could no longer hide from. She ground her hips hard into the seat to keep herself impacted. She tried to hold back her come, but the excitement, the intense heat of the pressure, was too much for her. She let out a huge, hopeless cry of lust and let go of herself. She shuddered and shook as she popped like a string of firecrackers in every direction. She moaned and groaned and tossed herself around the chair as she felt the waves of hot, blinding orgasm cover her. She spent herself hard onto the seat cushion; she thudded up and down in a thousand tiny hot jolts of electricity as she let go of her insides. Her come burst forth from deep inside her. It wracked her whole frame as she beat her clit harder and harder to keep up with the pace of the onslaught of her climax. She was coming like a truck barreling down a hill, and she couldn't stop herself. Furthermore, she didn't want to.

*

Vicky heard the buzz of her intercom and leaned forward to depress one of the call buttons. No doubt that was her secretary, Miss Schultz. Miss Harris had probably arrived. That was good. She needed Miss Harris. She needed a cute, sexy girl, the kind Bobby Dune had described over the phone. A girl who was hopelessly not cut out to be a secretary. A desperate girl. The girl was adorable. With sandy blonde locks that hung in curl clusters around her angelic-looking face. Those rosy cheeks, that teasing little smile. And those phenomenal-looking knockers. Her legs were well-proportioned, too, with tiny, chiseled ankles.

"Pleased to meet you, Miss West," Jane said, looking around to see if anything was amiss – nothing so far. And this woman, this Miss West, was so beautiful. For a moment, she thought she had walked into a modeling agency.

"Make that Vicky," the woman said, rising out of her seat and going to pull a chair over closer to her desk for the girl.

"Oh!" Jane replied, feeling quite at home despite the rather harsh-sounding tone in the woman's voice.

"Bobby told me you might be a suitable applicant for Temporary Secretary," the woman said, beaming across to her from the safety of her desk seat.

"I hope I'm a suitable applicant for something!" Jane said,

her words rushing uncontrollably past her teeth and out her mouth.

She would have liked to hold back a little on this woman and would like to have not revealed her pressing need for a job, her financial disability, and the fact that she needed to pay her rent one of these months. She would have liked to act suave, aloof, and cool. But she had already blown it a little with those first few words. So why the hell not come clean and blurt out the whole horrible mess? The worst the woman could do would be to send her away, and so many employers and agencies had done that already. She felt that she was walking around under a cursed rain cloud.

"Oh, Miss West .... uh, Vicky," the girl sobbed through clenched teeth, trying to control herself, "I'm so afraid."

"What's wrong?" the woman said, scanning the girl's entire body for any flaws, skin eruptions, or disabilities. The customers didn't like such things.

"I don't know, exactly," she wailed, fumbling in her purse for a handkerchief. As usual, she couldn't find one.

"Here," Vicky said, offering her a large box of tissues, "take one."

Jane reached up and tried to smile through her tears as she grabbed about fifteen tissues out of the hole of the white box. She felt like she needed a good cry, and she hoped the woman would be sympathetic.

"I can't seem to hold down a job," she said, wincing at the hard truth. It hurt not to be successful. It hurts not to be appreciated for your abilities. And it hurt to have to tell about it, too. But she felt like she was in the right place. At least the woman hadn't yet stood up and shoved her out of the office door.

"It happens," Vicky said calmly, running a fingernail through her long, winding hair. It was immaculate, but the girl was making her nervous.

"My mother told me I should have some kind of training, and I went to school," Jane revealed as she blew her nose. "St. Giles. I'm sure you heard of it."

Vicky had; it was one of those secretarial schools that sent her dozens of applicants when she worked for a regular job-finding agency. Their girls all acted like blown-up dolls and continued to wear their skirts short long after that style had gone the way of the bustle.

"I did like they said," she whimpered, dabbing at her eyes, "I wore my skirts short. I even learned to type and file. Shorthand, you know all the things I'm supposed to know about. And I actually graduated. But it's been downhill ever since."

"Care to talk about it," Vicky ventured, knowing the answer fully by this time.

"I've just been from pillar to post and back again in the two years since I graduated," she said, fighting hard to control the tears again. "I tried all different kinds of agencies, ads, job-finders places. And the offices. Absolutely everything. Lawyers, doctors, veterinarians, loan sharks, gypsies, pirates, you name it. They all seemed so nice in the beginning. I really got my hopes up for most of those jobs. I tried to get along with the office personnel and keep my nose clean. But always, always, inevitably, I got the sack."

The tears had started to run down again, and Jane found herself wiping her cheeks free of them as she tried to look up at Miss West and give her the whole story.

"You've had quite an ordeal," the dark-haired woman said, opening a drawer and pulling out her nail file. It was going to be a lengthy confession, so she figured it best not to waste time.

"The last man I worked for, Mr. Brook. It lasted three and a half days. He was a corker, all right. He treated me like I was a billboard for laxatives during working hours, but after five o'clock..." the girl's voice trailed off, and she shook her head, "he turned into the Cassanova of Thirty-Fourth Street. He invited me into this huge playroom; you wouldn't believe it. A bar, a revolving bar, actually, and a waterfall. A waterfall! Now, you would think I would have known that he didn't have anything on his mind other than, you know what!"

Vicky filed her nails and blew at them a little. This girl obviously had an overactive imagination. That was all to the good. But she also talked too much.

"Miss Harris, Jane, if you don't mind," she said, very motherly, very smoothly, as she grinned like a diabolical banshee, "I'd like to hear your story, but I trust you understand that I have other clients waiting to see me. It sounds like you have had the unfortunate circumstance that many young girls find themselves in. You're attractive, bright," she swallowed hard and continued, "and in need of some specialized placement. And we here at Temporary Secretary Temps are experts in specialized placement. We specialize in it."

"Do you really think you can find me a place, Vicky?" Jane said, staring hopefully into the woman's amber eyes.

"I think we can," the woman answered, "but it's going to take a little work. There's never a fee at Temporary Secretary Temps; we prefer to take a percentage. Off the top."

"I don't care about the money," Jane lied, "I want a job."

"Now, now," Miss West said, shaking a sharply-pointed finger at Jane, "don't be so anxious to sound humanitarian. There's nothing wrong with money. It's human to want to be paid for one's labor."

"How much would I make, do you think," she dared to ask, "provided, of course, you could place me?"

"More than you've been able to make through any other agency," the woman sat back and smiled as she swiveled her chair from one side to the other. "We guarantee it."

"I only hope I can live up to your expectations, Miss West, Vicky," the blonde girl answered. She sniffled a little and pocketed the remaining fistful of tissues.

"We will have to test you, of course," the woman said, sounding very officious suddenly.

It was what Jane had been waiting for. She would test anywhere from average to dismal if her past record could be trusted. She stuck her dimpled knees together and sat straighter in the chair.

"I'm ready," she said, bringing two fingers to her forward and giving a little salute.

Miss West smiled patronizingly and stood up. "This won't be the usual kind of test, Jane."

"Oh?" the girl said, looking for signs from Miss West's composure and movements as to what that might mean. She found none.

"We are looking for a certain 'je ne sais quoi', a certain quality in our girls that will help them please our very demanding, very particular clients. So our testing methods may initially seem a little peculiar to you."

"Mr. Dune told me they might," she said, feeling more confident than she had a right to.

"Yes," the woman said, in a voice dripping with honey and butter, "would you come right this way?"

Vicky steered the lost lamb to her closet and opened it a crack. She flipped the mirrored door over against itself, and Jane saw her whole figure reflected there in the glass.

"I'm going to give you a little test now." Vicky cooed to her. "Let's see how you do."

Jane held her breath and steadied herself. It might be tough, but she would give it her best shot.

Vicky reached into the closet and grabbed three separate outfits off their hangars. She walked briskly to the wide sofa along one wall of the room and laid them out along it. Jane saw her set down a frilly summer dress with a pair of white gloves and a flowered pocketbook. Next, she put down a slinky, satin sheath dress with a plunging neckline and silver heels with ankle straps. The third piece was a black patent leather mini skirt with a studded corset attached, full Wellington black leather boots with laces up the front, and a cat of nine tails.

Vicky moved away from the display and paced up and down the room for a few seconds before speaking.

"Jane," she said, sounding like a regal monarch about to issue a royal decree, "supposing a client calls you and wants you to come to work for him. He says he needs a nice girl who minds her own business and can type, file, take dictation, and act very sweet to him. Under these circumstances, which outfit would you select?"

Without hesitation, Jane pointed to the frilly white smock dress.

"So far, so good," Vicky said, continuing her little pacing trip, only speeding up a bit.

"Now, supposing a client calls. He wants a smart girl who knows how to take care of business and doesn't mind working late. She need not be able to type, file, or answer a telephone. Given these requirements, which ensemble here would you pick?"

Jane thought a moment. She wanted to make the right decision.

"Uh," she said, thinking it over carefully, "that one." She had pointed to the tight black sheath satin thing.

"Excellent," Miss West snapped. "Now, Jane, for the third and most difficult part of the test." She brought her hands behind her back and continued pacing like a college professor lecturing on electro-physics.

"The telephone rings. It's a plaintive, yearning voice. A client. He wants a strong, clever girl. One who can mind her own business and everybody else's. She should be able to take charge. To give orders. But most of all, she should be able to discipline a man. Tell me, which costume would you wear on such an assignment?"

Jane began to pace, too. She bit her nail and scratched her arm. This wasn't as easy as it looked in the beginning. Now, the questions were getting really tough. She would have to put the old thinking cap on to get this one right.

"There," she said finally, pointing her finger to the frilly flowered dress, "that one. I'd wear that one."

Miss West stared at her like she was Mr. Stanley encountering Dr. Livingston in the jungles of Africa. "Why?" she asked crisply.

"Well," Jane said, twirling on one foot and feeling pretty proud of herself, "you said, 'discipline,' and that dress reminds me of my third-grade teacher, Miss Prendergast. Christ, could that lady wield a ping-pong paddle!"

Jane looked up at Miss West, walking back toward the window. She said nothing for a moment, then turned to face the girl full front.

"Very well, Miss Harris!" she said firmly and loudly, "I think you're ready for the second phase of our testing. Let's hope you do better than you did on the first."

3 – Paying Overdue Rent

The petite brunette pulled open the dresser drawer in the corner of her bedroom and fumbled around for something tight. Anything tight. Her hand grasped a pair of tight pedal pushers, and she yanked them out, bringing half the drawer's contents with her.

”Shit,” she said as she gathered the stuff and stuck it back in the drawer. She was about to dig in the clothes hamper for something more appealing than a pair of gray pedal pushers with a hole in the crotch, no matter how tight they may be, when she remembered that her roommate had a few figure-hugging things. She shoved the door shut and headed toward her room.

”Fucking no account bitch better keep something clean in there,” she said to the empty hallway, knowing that she couldn't manage to keep anything clean at all. Probably came from doing your laundry once every six months, she figured, as she turned the knob to her friend's bedroom.

Fortunately, Jane wasn't home. She had gone job-looking. She did that practically twice a week. So even though she wasn't working much, she was gone a lot. It was a nice arrangement. Emma hadn't published a poem in about a year and had had to take in typing from the local university to make ends meet. And now, with Jane out of work, she was trying to make both ends meet. And it wasn't working out too well.

She opened the blonde girl's closet and slid a few hangers

around. There, hanging limply off one of them, was a lavender jumpsuit. Made of sheerest stretch nylon, it had to be better than anything she could find in her room. She lifted it off the hanger, happy to have found something soft and sexy at last.

Lavender matched her eyes, too. They were blue, with just a hint of something darker in them. Probably devilishness. Emma and Jane had been roommates since Jane got out of secretarial school, and Emma finished bartending school. Their schools were on the same block. Right around the corner, in fact. Emma had so much trouble making martinis and figuring out what a Harvey Wallbanger was supposed to have in it that she almost dropped out, but finally did manage to graduate. The girls started a conversation one day under a cafe umbrella in the park, shared lunch, and became good friends in no time. They shared a lot. Neither of them could seem to find their niche in the world. They both felt they were failures, accidents waiting to happen. Or maybe it was just that their time hadn't come yet.

Emma popped her sexy, petite figure into the slithering jumpsuit and pulled the thing up. She couldn't afford to wear underwear today. Excess baggage. Besides, she wanted Mr. Perry to see every ridge on her nipple, every wisp of her luscious auburn bush patch. She couldn't afford to have him miss a thing. The girls owed him a whopping bill in back rent.

She looked at herself in Jane's dresser mirror and arched her back hard. Her tits made lovely high rounds of delectable flesh under the material, and they strained hard against it, threatening to burst out of the zipper. Her thighs hugged in there tightly, too, creating the impression that she had been poured into the thing. Or she wasn't really wearing material, just a coat of thick paint. That was what she wanted.

"Bitch better not bitch 'cause I got her clothes on," she said aloud as she turned to profile and patted her pert little backside. You could see everything inside that suit. "She owes half the back rent, after all."

Her doorbell buzzed as she picked up a hairbrush. Her long, straight chestnut hair would just have to wait.

She then checked her flawless make-up in the mirror. She seldom wore it. Her face was such a naturally adorable, radiant little mask; she didn't need that kind of enhancement, but today, well, today was different. Today, in less than a minute, she would go to that door and let Mr. Perry in. And she was going to screw him. She was going to screw him for the back rent.

"Hi, Matthew," she said as she opened the door and peeked shyly into the hall. She had let part of her long, silky hair fall across her forehead, seductively hiding part of one eye.

Mr. Perry was unused to hearing his tenants call him by his first name. In fact, he had no idea she even knew what it was.

"Hello, Miss Mccarthy," the man said curtly. He stepped inside and looked around. The girls had kept the place well enough, no nails in the wall or pets. If only they had paid their rent on time, he wouldn't have to evict them. It hurt him to do that. And it cost him money, but his course was set. His wife had been nagging him about it all week.

"Won't you come in?" she said, going for the lower registers of her husky voice. It was lucky she had that kind of voice.

And it was lucky she looked a lot older than her twenty-one years, whereas her roommate looked a lot younger than hers.

Mr. Perry sailed past her and stood with his hands in his lap as though she were about to say a benediction.

Emma gritted her teeth and tried to ignore what she knew was coming next.

"I guess you know why I'm here, Miss Mccarthy," the man said, rocking back onto his heels. He hated throwing tenants out, especially two girls as cute and sexy as these roommates, but his wife left him no choice.

"Let me guess," she said, wiggling her hot ass all the way over to where he was standing, "but if we're going to talk about it, please call me Emma." Emma stared hard at the short man rocking back and forth on the throw rug. He was slightly balding, wore horn-rimmed glasses, and smelled like moldy violets. But he had been friendly to her and Jane, up to now, only made one phone call to remind them they were in arrears with the rent money and had generally let them do their own thing and stayed pretty much out of their way. She wondered if she could seduce him in five minutes.

"Emma," the man began ceremoniously, "I'm afraid I'm going to have to give you an ultimatum."

"Oh, Matthew," the girl said, easing her way down onto the sofa across from where he stood, feeling her way with her hands, "I hope you won't be too harsh with me. It's been a long day, and I've had so much work."

"I know you're a hard-working girl, Emma," the man said dourly, "I know because the neighbors are complaining about your typewriter going all night. But that does not alter the basic issue."

"Which is?" Emma said, twisting a little piece of her copper hair between her fingers and crossing her legs. They were covered, but he could have seen the brand name if she had a bandaid on her knee.

"Please, Emma," the man said, feeling hot under his collar. It was difficult being a stern landlord in these surroundings. They should be in his office, with his wife in the reception room, but here, with all this soft furniture and this soft little kitten purring up at him from the sofa.

"Aren't you going to sit down?" the girl asked, patting the sofa seat beside her. "We can talk better if you do. I've got a big thing for eye contact."

Matthew Perry was developing a big thing for eye contact, too. Especially with that one eye of hers, the one he could see. The other one was hidden behind long tresses of spun gold and copper. He wanted to press that luscious metal into his palms. He tried to control himself as he sat down.

"I'm going to be frank. You owe me four hundred and fifty-five dollars and forty-seven cents. I have my bills to pay, too. I need the money. I'm not a healthy man, though I know I look fit enough. I have children in college, they need a grand a week. Bills, constant upkeep and repair of this place, and that's not to mention...." He broke off as he found himself staring very closely into Emma Mccarthy's lucid, batting blue eyes.

"I never noticed that before," she said in her throatiest, most ardent voice.

”Noticed what?” he said, slightly annoyed at being caught off guard.

”Your dimple.”

”This?” the man said, pointing to a little impression on one side of his cheek. ”This is not a dimple. It's a war wound.”

Emma threw her gorgeous head back and laughed in her most cunning and gurgling manner.

”What's so funny?” the man asked behind his thick glasses.

”I was just wondering if you would show me where it came out!” Emma said, lifting her head upright and licking her lips.

Matthew chuckled momentarily and brought his hand down to his knee to find Emma Mccarthy's hand already rested there. He felt himself suddenly hopelessly given over to this girl. She was so captivating. So animal. So warm and sensual. And her tits were so big!

”So what is it, Emma?” the man said, straightening his tie. ”You trying to screw me for the back rent?”

Emma felt a protest rise up in her throat but squelched it hard. Then she arched her back as hard as she could without cracking her spine and nodded in the naughtiest fashion she could find.

”Well, I don't think we should be doing it in the living room,” the man said, patting the firm fingers that rested on his knee, now making their way toward his thigh. He figured they had about another four inches to go before they would meet head-on with his pent-up schlong, which was crashing around its cotton cage like a snake on amphetamines.

Emma grinned at him and spidered her fingers up higher toward his cock basket.

"Why don't you take that thing down a little further and let me see you?" the man said, his breath drawing in with increasing difficulty.

Emma reached up and slowly worked the tight zipper down. She had only about an inch and a half to go before her full moons would come bouncing up out of the suit. When they did so, Matthew gasped.

"God, that's a gorgeous sight," he said, stretching his hands out and reaching for her round, bouncing pair.

He squirmed hard as he made contact with the milky flesh of her tit loaves. They were incredibly voluptuous, soft, springy, and solid. He brought his mouth down and sucked one nipple hard between his teeth. It rose up like a bun in an oven. He gobbled, slurped, and pried his teeth around the circumference of her lustrous, bumpy nipples. He let his tongue circle them, play all the way around her whole tit, then slide into the succulent valley between and play with her crevice, then onto the other tit, around and around again. He could feel the moisture building up on them. He was getting them slick and juicy from his greedy, lapping tongue.

He's not much to look at, Emma thought as she felt her knobs rising to meet his probing tongue, but he sure can suck a tit!

The man felt his angry wand flail against his zipper track. He felt his huge, caged monster ramming and slamming up and down his underwear basket. He knew he would have to get some relief, and soon.

Just as he was about to let it out, Emma reached down and patted it.

"That feels like it wants out," she cooed like a turtle dove. "May I?"

"Oh, God, I hope so," the middle-aged man replied. His glasses had become foggy, and he let them down over his nose.

"You're hung like a horse," the girl purred, stroking his hard whang. "I'd like to wrap my lips around that."

Without another word, she slipped out from under his huge hands and slithered to the floor in neat sections. She grabbed the metal tab on his zipper and worked it down slowly, tooth by tooth.

"This is exciting!" she said as she reached in and pulled out his stiff prick.

She was really unsure of what she would find in there. The man was such a small guy. About five foot and four inches. Maybe shorter. But he had broad shoulders and a king-sized nose, so no telling. But she was unprepared for the hairy monster she pulled out of his dark cave.

"Economy size!" she said, wondering where she was going to put it after she got it out.

The man sat back and felt more confident. He saw the girl looking down at his big rod and felt relaxed and amused. His wife had never acted very impressed with his cock, but this girl was taking in the sights and admiring them.

"You've got a whang on you, Sir!" she said, surveying the hard log in her hands. "I just hope we can find a suitable spot for it."

The man shrugged his shoulders and tried to act nonchalant.

"How about your ass?" he said offhandedly.

"Huh?" Emma said, wondering how she would be able to get both hands wrapped around it at once.

"Like I said, Emma, you owe a lot of back rent."

"Oh," the girl said, feeling as defeated as Napoleon at Waterloo.

"You should get it nice and wet first, though," he smiled, removing his glasses for the first time since early morning and setting them on the end table. "I don't want you to get hurt."

Emma sat like a statue until the man coughed a little and reminded her that she had his prick in her hand by pointing toward it. And what a huge, wild dick it was. She couldn't tell how many inches exactly, but she doubted her mouth would go around it.

She started working the head, where she knew most of the action was. That might make him wet, at least. She spat on her fingers and slid them back and forth delicately across the wide knob of his cock tip. She worked the milky droplets of pre-cum around the whole circumference of his big dome and slid all five fingers around in it. She brought her other hand up and, opposing her fingers and thumb, clung to the rim while she continued to play the dome with her fingers. It wasn't long before low, long moans came out of his mouth.

"Ohh," he groaned, unable to remember the last time his wife had felt him up this way. The heat of arousal was making his collar wet.

"I hope you like a good hand job," she said, getting both her hands into the act. She had to use all the muscles all the way up to her armpits, but she figured she could jack him off to climax, at least.

"To a certain point," the man replied cocksurely.

Emma felt her heart sink into her slippers. This guy knew what he wanted, and he certainly had the purchasing power.

"You do that good," the man said, spreading his legs and watching the girl play around the rim and across the head of his massive hard salami.

"I want to do it good," Emma said in her sexiest, lustiest voice.

He knew she wanted to do it good till he spilled his prick juice down her hand, but he also knew he had staying power. He hadn't been married twenty-six years to a frigid marine sergeant for nothing.

Emma let her gripping fingers slide down onto his shaft. It was tough, leathery, and hard. The skin was wrinkly and deeply-veined. The entire length of it was as hard as an elephant's hide. And totally intriguing. How had this little shrimp sprung such a massive cock anyhow?

Matthew watched the girl's sure fingers slip down over his cock hood and slide along the shaft. They made their way down tightly and rammed against his balls a little as they hit the hilt. Then she brought them up again, and he felt his belt buckle melt. This girl was turning him on like crazy.

"Take that thing off," he managed out his yellow tobacco-stained teeth, "I want to see your twat, you know."

Emma continued playing up and down his thick, greasy, hard shaft as she worked the jumpsuit down over her hips. Then she wiggled her butt out of the tight sticking thing and thrashed at it with her feet until it came off all the way.

"Now stand up," he said, "but keep playing with me. I love it."

And he did. Her sure, small hands were playing symphonies of mixed notes and rhythms against his wracking schlong. Sweeter than any music he had heard in a long time.

Emma was masturbating him quite rapidly now. She sailed her hands up high and brought them down fast as she stood between her legs and bent over.

Matthew felt his shaft oozing come. It felt like vanilla icing dripping off a hot cupcake. He felt the girl's long, silky strands of head hair dangling and brushing against his thighs as she stood there and jerked him, beating his hard, heavy, pulsating meat. The sights, the sounds, the smells were engulfing him.

Emma was sure she could get him to come if only she would be allowed a few more minutes of this beating action. She felt her own bush burning a little as she spread her legs and allowed the man's hands between them.

He brought them up to her pussy lips and began rubbing them together with his fat, forceful fingers. She heard them clack like railroad cars along the tracks. She felt the sweet oozing of some joy juice slip out from between her thick, pink lips. The man knew what he was doing all right. She wondered who he'd been practicing on.

"Come up on my lap, Little Girl," the man said in a forced, fatherly voice. "Come up and see what Daddy has here."

She edged toward the sofa, bent one knee up, and brought it down on one side of him. Then, balancing on that one, and with the help of his firm hand circling her waist, she lifted the other one off the floor and slapped it down on his other side.

She sat there with her knees spread wide, her cunt pointing to within inches from the man's rocking, reeling hard schlong point.

She lowered her cunt down and spread her moist, hot pussy lips apart. She entwined his throbbing pecker pole with them and rubbed it to get both of them hot from the friction.

"Oohh," the man said, rolling his eyes back and thrusting his hips high up off the chair. "That's a lot of something. I can't figure out what."

He chuckled a little and felt his temperature rise another ten degrees. He played with the girl's hot tits as she bounced on her knees and rode her cunt lips along his prick and around the head. Tip to lips. It was a satisfying juxtaposition.

Emma was about to sink right down onto the man's flailing pecker stick, slide right over his greased cock pole, but as she got into position to do so, unable to hold herself back much longer, like it or not, he braced her around the waist with his huge hands and stopped her in her tracks.

"Huh, uh, Honey," he said, shaking his big sorrowful head at her, "remember, up your ass."

Emma was about to protest when he lifted her up smart and plopped her down again so that her oozing brown sphincter was touching the crown of his fuck stick.

"Oh, golly," was all she managed to utter as he began working the flat part of cock dome up around her brown and pink anus muscle. "I don't see how that's ever going to go in."

"Watch," the man said, bringing a handful of spit and saliva around and caressing his dick with it. "And listen."

He pulled the girl's legs hard apart with his hands and stuck his hips high up into the air. He worked his slimy throbbing head up into the tightly resisting shit vent and kept wiggling it hard until it made a little headway right in there.

"Oww!" Emma called out, wishing to hell her glorious roommate could be here to share her half of the expenses about now.

"God, you're tight," said the little man with the big dick.

He rode his stiff prick right up inside her bunghole. He pressed his fleshy loaf past her anal sphincter and right up into her poop chute. He worked his hot, hard, heaving, heavy prick tip along her gripping sphincter wall and up her ass. He pumped his big, red meat pole inside her. He thrust his hips up and down and fucked the shit right out of her.

"Gawd," he screamed as he felt his cock tingling at every pore, the hot lust welling up inside his bowels.

"Oww," Emma let out of her clenched teeth in a rush of pain and pleasure. The little man's prick was turning her on so hard and so bad and so completely she had to grab her own clit between her fingers to relieve the pain.

"Fuck here it comes," the man said, screwing his cock hard into her butt. "I'm gonna blow my top." He rocked hard up inside her and let go of his man load in one swift kick of the bucket. He shot his jism trail up high into her bowels and poured his spunk portion all over her hot, wiggling insides. The tightness of the place, the grip of her ass muscles, the heat from her bowels. He was fucking the fiery pits of hell. No, he was the fiery pits of hell. He was the devil. He was the devil, and he was fucking like the devil.

Again and again and again, the man brought his pecker up

inside Emma's hot white ass hole. It felt like a poker sending live sparks up inside her bunghole. She couldn't get her air. She was gasping for breath and riding the man's big pecker log for all she could stand. She grabbed her clit and beat it intently. She brought her fingers to her love button and pushed non-stop as the man plugged her ass hole. She rode him hard and jerked herself off to a climax as she felt the sting of the man's piercing blade slide in and out her hot ass cheeks.

"Shit!" she hollered so loud a man working on the roof looked up, "I'm coming…" She whacked herself hard and firm and spilled her clear liquid joy juice out her cunt, out her ass, out her mouth.

Every fiber of her being was screaming with rage, pain, desire, lust, and heat. She came in every direction. Every muscle worked together, then in opposition to release her of her come load. She came hard as she rode the man's big prick down to her butt hilt.

4 – The Married Couple

Chloe Keating brought the hard leather bullwhip swiftly down to her husband's bare red bottom. He writhed and squealed in pain.

"Eat me, Slave!" she said as she grabbed a handful of his curly black hair and yanked his head back hard enough to make him choke.

"Agh," he replied, knowing full well that he hadn't a chance of wheedling his way out of this one. No matter how much he begged, no matter how much he pleaded, she was going to have her way with him.

The woman hooked one thumb around her black studded corset loops and leaned back. God, she loved playing that stiff old bull whip crop in her hand. And the fine, crisp snapping sound the whip made when it struck the still air. It sent shivers and chills down her spine. Her husband knelt humbly at her feet. He looked so forlorn and pathetic kneeling down there on all fours, like a dog.

"Suck my pussy, Shit Face!" she said, rudely jerking her cunt into his face. She had him locked right where she wanted him all right. Strung up to the doorknob on one side of the room and tied to the bedpost on the other. And she had his head locked into a black cowhide collar with a thick silver ring sticking out of it. And on that ring hung a single silver chain. The one she was using right now to jerk his head toward her.

The man felt his face growing flush red and purple as the

woman led him by the neck, closer ever closer to outstretched pulsating pussy lips. They were so red and round and quivering. Her slit was so enormous, thrust up there against his face. He felt that he might be pulled right in, head and all, if she didn't ease up on that chain she was leading him by.

"Vile, Disgusting Filth Monkey!!! " she crowed at him as she felt the hot tingling sensation of local arousal permeate her pussy meat.

"You don't deserve to draw another breath. You only live because I have not yet decided whether I shall snuff out your wretched life or allow you to continue on here as my lowly slave."

"Anything," the man gasped, fighting for the air which was choking off his throat. "Anything you desire, Mistress."

"I saw you," she said, mocking him cruelly, "I saw you watching that lousy piece of ass, that dumb cunt head of a bitch sitting across from us tonight. She almost made me want to puke in my dinner!"

"I humbly beg you, Mistress," the man said, shaking his head and letting his dark lashes flutter together. The pain was circling his neck like a vise. "I beg you to reconsider. Please, please forgive me. I am humbly and truly sorry to have ever offended you in any way. I live only to serve you."

Then Lucas Keating closed his eyes and pressed his lips together. The chills that ran down his spine were as real as the pain running round his neck, squeezing the breath out of him.

"I'm not ready to make my decision yet," the woman said, brandishing the whip high in the air and snapping it a good one before she brought it down firmly across his raised raw butt. "You will have to wait until my pleasure has been taken care of before I decide whether to let you live or die!"

With those words, the whip came crashing through space again, splitting the air like a gunshot and wallopping Lucas's hot, quivering buttocks.

Chloe leaned back and let her legs flop out. God, she loved the way her cunt looked from up here. So wide and pink and wet and ready. Ready for her pleasure. Ready for her slave's obedience to it.

Her breasts were pushed high up over the top of the tight stay-fastened corset, and she could see her nipples bulging out from the tips of them. They looked like snow-covered peaks with volcanic ash clinging to the tops. They made her hotter and hornier still if such a thing were possible, just looking down at them.

Her husband had been a bad boy that night. Very bad. And he would have to be punished. She closed her eyes and thought back to the events of that night.

The dinner party had started out normally enough. Ten guests. Not a big affair, as those things went, but lavish. Like all of Chloe's dinner parties. This one was given for her girlfriend, who had just announced that she was going.

"The table looks lovely," Samantha, her girlfriend, told her as she waltzed into the room. "God, Chloe, I'm so excited. Jack's bringing his sister here tonight, and I haven't even met her."

Chloe looked at her friend, a little annoyed. Jack's sister was not on the list of dinner guests. She would have to set an extra place for her somewhere. And that would make an uneven number. Tacky, in the circles she frequented.

Chloe and Lucas Keating were gifted. Even by their friends' standards, they had been both born into families of means. Chloe's family had been 'old money', a family whose forefathers made a bundle in real estate. Jack's family was nouveau riche, a bunch of farmers, as far back as Jack knew, until his father got lucky and struck it rich when he opened a fast food chicken wing stand. That little venture just took off and made Jack's father a millionaire in less than five years.

They met at college. Jack was attracted by Chloe's physical attributes at first. The strawberry blonde hair, the lush body, the freckled smile. And Chloe was turned on by Jack. He was so dark and mysterious looking. He was such a big, handsome hunk of man. Boy, actually, but she could see the potential. She found out his family had money, and the match was instantaneous. And it had proved a good one over the last four years. They liked many of the same things, including heavy dominance and bondage.

And right now, Jack was getting his daily dose. He worshipped that long, tall willow of a woman. She was such a tower of strength. Worked out alongside him every day in their own private gymnasium. She could lift a lot of weight for a woman. They designed that gymnasium together. And less than six months later, they designed their own torture chamber.

It was everything they had both come to love. Complete with stone floor, stocks, pillories, slave auction block, manacles and shackles tied into the wall, and leather accouterments of every size, shape, and description. And they got about as much use out of that room as they did the gym.

"Unworthy Lowlife!" Chloe hissed as the whip stung the man's hard, driven buttocks. His crevice was running with the sweat of pain and arousal. But the leather studded chastity belt he wore did not allow for him to take his throbbing, aching schlong out. It was firmly held against his flat, hard stomach until such time as his Mistress would lean over and unzip him. She only did that when she was good and ready. The build-up, though, was pure heaven.

Just thinking of that snotty blonde bitch made Chloe crack her whip harder. How dare she invade their lovely home with not even so much as an invitation. And that disgusting lime dress she had on! It was a cheap display of obscene sex if Chloe had ever seen it. If she hadn't been her best friend's fiance's sister. Christ! She would have that bitch down here, too, right now, licking the polish off her boots. The thought of that drove Chloe wild with frenzied sexual lust. A woman slave! How quaint. How exciting. Up to now, she had used men, primarily her husband. But, then, they were new at this.

"I wouldn't take that pouty-mouthed bitch to a shit fight and use her as a shield!" she said in a low, buzzing voice as she sailed her whip through the air again and brought it right down on her husband's exposed left butt mound. She felt so proud of herself to be raising such tremendous red and raw-looking welts all along his backside. They looked like long strands of rubies laid against his flat, hard skin.

She yanked harder on the chain and brought her husband's mouth up to the very ridges of her cunt lips.

"Now suck, Creep!" she said in a stiff, Skene's voice, "Suck, or I'll whip you to hamburger!"

The man knew it was time to be allowed to suck those sweet, pulsating pussy lips. Those big, circling ridges of puffy desire. Those wet, hot, luscious wedges of tart, tantalizing goodness.

He opened his slobbering, slavering lips and emitted his tongue. It went out like a red, wet snake looking for a place to strike. It curled up hard like the tongue of a chameleon before he struck his wife's juicy red prey.

"Ahh," she cried in ecstasy as the man's rolled-up log slapped against her pussy lips. "Suck me, Slave Man!" she whispered in hot, writhing lust.

Lucas Keating ran his thick, obedient tongue all around the rim of his wife's delicious red honey hole. He prodded and poked his assertive wet weapon up into her cunt crack and diddled her clit with it. She writhed and moaned in pleasure as he did so.

He felt so completely under her power. Totally controlled by her every whim and snap of the whip. And he felt quite happy to serve her. To be at her every beck and call. He was glad he had flirted with that girl, Jack's sister, whatever her name was. She was a tart, all right. And she had been making an obvious play for Lucas.

He was used to those things. Most women he could leave alone without the slightest notion of following through with any of them once they came on to him. He had no desire whatsoever to play around or act unfaithfully to his wife in thought, word, or deed. He was totally devoted to her. Her willing and obedient slave. Her total and complete subservient servant. Her lowly footstool, if that is what she wished.

He felt the woman's feet rise up and come down around his broad shoulders.

"Fuck me with your tongue, Disgusting Worm!" the woman said, spitting down her words like steel from a staple gun. "Fuck me with your hopeless little mouth pecker."

She threw her head back and laughed cruelly as he continued to probe and prod her clit and crack with his vibrating, slimy red working tongue.

His knees rubbed briskly against the carpet of their bedroom floor. They were bruised and raw from having been on all fours for so long, but he didn't care. He could only feel the ramming, cramming of his tongue muscle up her pussy. The throbbing, weaving pattern cut across her rigid cunt lips and down all the way to her ass button.

Chloe thrust her butt hole right up at him and ordered him to stick his face in it.

"Kiss my ass, Shark Bait!" she seethed through mean, clenched white teeth.

The man caressed her bunghole with his tongue and bathed it in all the liquid he could possibly muster. He washed and scoured the shit right out of her ass with each thrust of his eager, prodding tongue. He scooped up the shit out of the luscious ass vent and felt his insides grow heavy and fluttery at the ecstasy of the taste of her.

"Oh, Mistress," he cried, "I'll do anything, anything to serve you."

"Ream my butt, Dog! ' she scolded, letting her whip find

its natural home again. The welts across his buttocks were raising to a fine red shine.

The man reamed and poked and lapped at his wife's ass hole. His cock was growing so stiff he thought it might split the leather and metal of his chastity belt. That lovely little belt with its tight jock and its bare butt holes. She had bought it for him, this woman he adored.

The woman felt herself grow hot to the point of itchiness with arousal. She reached down and masturbated her clit hard as the man continued to eat out her bunghole. He plugged her ass with his tongue and took his shit medicine right down his gullet. He burrowed up deeply and brought his tongue out again. He loved every shit-licking second of it.

Chloe flicked her clit still harder with her ever-ready fingers. It was growing hot and hard under her grasp. The tingling, reaming sensation of the tongue to butt hole was driving her right out of her seat. She lifted her hips up, bracing her weight against her husband's shoulders.

How dare he! After all, she thought, as she worked her fingers faster than beavers chewing wood for a dam, who did he think he was smiling and winking at that insipid pale little mouse of a girl sitting across from him. And to think she had only seated her there because there was no other place for her to sit. Damn! Uneven numbers at her dining room table always made for trouble!

She stuck her butt higher into her husband's face. Let him choke on my ass hole! She thought that might be nice. Let him drown in my come juice, she thought as she continued the speeded-up process of fingering herself ever harder and feeling her clit grow ever harder and twanging against her flailing cunt lips.

”Ream me, Faithless One!” she said, throwing her head back and shaking her clit still harder.

Lucas locked his tongue up inside her butt vent. The slippery brown tunnel of her ass hole delighted him beyond description. His cock banged angrily against its leather and steel cage.

Chloe felt herself ready, ready, and on the edge of her canyon of desire. She reached around with her clit massaging hand and unhooked the silver rivet that kept her slave's member inside. The thing bounced out like a log down a sawmill falls. His enormous rock-hard pecker was slamming and whamming hard against the chastity belt and against his stomach. And soon, she knew for sure, it would be ramming against her, too.

”Now, Slave!” she commanded as she slid even further down into the chair and clasped her muscular thighs hard against her husband's neck.

He reared up off his raw haunches and speared her cunt hole savagely with his hot, hard sword prick. He impaled her on his punishing cock rod. He humped and shoved and sweated and shoved and humped and sweated and insinuated his giant cock right down into her seething, writhing pussy tunnel. Chloe gripped him tightly around the neck and let him pound the daylights out of her. No man under his own steam could fuck like this; she knew that for a fact. No man could possibly screw this way unless he had been brought to the brink with insane torture and teasing beyond human endurance. "Fuck me."

"Fuck that hole!"

"Stick that pole down in there and fuck my pussy, Slave Boy."

"Fuck me."

"Fuck my pussy."

"Fuck that wet hole with your big bone, your big wet throbbing bone!"

Lucas Keating gave her such a drilling his peter felt like a corkscrew. He slammed down on her again and again and again. He brought his pecker out to the very lips of her clit and held it there a breathless, priceless moment. Then he slammed it back in and drove the cunt's cunt hole all the way to a hard, fast, dizzy climax.

He felt her go off under him like a barrel of gunpowder. She exploded beneath his thrusting, humping schlong like the Chinese New Year.

"Ooh," she said as she lit up and headed skyward.

Then Lucas felt himself flinging his guts out the end of his prick. His cock hole opened up and let his come load out in heavy, huge geyser jets. He shot his man load hard into his wife's waiting, tight, hot cunt. He flung his come juice all up inside her wet pink tunnel and then yanked himself out of her throbbing hole. He spread the rest of his man-come all over her lustrous strawberry blonde bush. He smeared it right in with his still rock-hard pecker. He felt like an artist making a masterpiece with his tool.

Then he sat back and watched in complete awe and worship

as his wife bent her head over and licked the delicious cream off her own heaving wet pussy mound.

Twenty minutes later, the two of them sat up in their king-size bed and talked like a couple of school kids.

"I was so jealous of that little bitch tonight, you bad, bad boy," the woman cooed, playing with the brushy hairs on his chest.

"I know," Lucas grinned as he brought his firm, strong fingers down on his wife's stuck-up red nipples. "You proved it later, too."

"I wished I had that toady little cunt right there next to you, Lucas," the woman said, wiggling her toes against her husband's foot. "I'd have made her my slave, too. That's what I would have done."

Lucas thought a moment. Maybe that might be fun. Add a new dimension to their little fun and games. But how would he fit in?

"I'd have tied her up and sat on her. Used some really stiff nylon cord and wrapped it down around her torso, and brought the end right tight over her big, sloppy cunt hole. That's just how I'd have done it."

Chloe thought a moment. Oh, it would be such fun to have herself a female slave. Someone they could both torture. A new little nubile slave girl to enhance the dominance and bondage. Such fun. Such fun just thinking about it.

"Darling," Lucas said, snuggling his hand closer to his wife's honey pot, "why don't we get ourselves such a person? Not Jack's sister, of course; she's much too close to Samantha for comfort. And I certainly wouldn't invite her to any parties of ours again. That lime dress was atrocious. But what about a really innocent, willing, trainable little slave girl?"

"One we could spank and paddle and tease and bind and torture?" his wife said brightly, sitting up a little and opening her eyes wide with the intriguing thought.

"Something like that," Lucas answered, "a fresh young thing. A little daisy out of an onion patch. A slave girl... Hmmm."

The thought tantalized him so much that he reached down to stroke his cock and think about it a little more. Not surprisingly, he found it already rock-hard.

5 – Ride Like a Horsie

"I mean it, Jane," Emma said, pulling the ice tray out of the refrigerator and clanking it down on the counter, "you should have been here."

Jane sat down on the kitchen chair and tried to resist a grin. She watched as her roommate banged half a dozen ice cubes out and wrapped one in an old blue washcloth. Then she reached up under her shortie pajamas and popped the terry cloth bundle onto her ass.

"At least you could have worked for your half of the rent," the girl said, feeling the rush of cold hit her swollen, raw ass hole. "I'm telling you, Kid, that old man has got a pecker on him the size of that egg beater."

Jane still had to squelch a laugh. She couldn't possibly imagine that old Matthew Perry was hung all that huge. He was such a little guy. A munchkin.

Emma eased herself down onto the kitchen chair and looked at the clock. "Ow," she said when her throbbing buttocks touched ground zero. "I feel like I have been sitting on the wrong end of a beanstalk."

"I'm sorry," Jane said, trying not to laugh out loud. "But I want you to know, you acted like a champ, fending that monster off and canceling our rent debt like that. You really were a brave warrior."

"I was a soft ass sucker what I was," Emma said, feeling the waves of pain rolling over her like a panzer division. "And our rent debt has not been canceled, not exactly. He would only agree to a postponement."

"I wish I could say and watch you take a Sitz bath, Em," Jane said, gazing up at the clock, "but I gotta go."

"What time are they making you report for work at that place," the girl said, rocking on her reddened butt hole from side to side.

"She said anytime as long as I'm there by nine," Jane said, strolling into the bedroom, trying like hell to decide what to wear. "Are you sure you got this job?" Emma said. Her roommate did not have a good track record as far as getting jobs was concerned. In fact, up until now, her track record hadn't even been on the track.

"Yes," Jane shouted back, "Miss West gave me several tests, and I finally passed one, but it was the most important one."

"Shorthand?" Emma shouted again, rubbing the ice cube against her anus so hard it was beginning to melt into a little suspicious-looking puddle onto the kitchen chair.

"No," Jane said, wishing to hell her roommate would keep her questions to herself. She certainly didn't feel like explaining the whole thing.

"Typing?" the girl called back, intrigued as to how her roommate had finally scored a job that sounded as promising as this one without even taking a shorthand test.

"No," Jane cried back, "have you seen my navy blue pumps?"

"Jane," Emma said, standing in her doorway, "what the hell did they test you for at this place... what's it called?"

"Temporary Secretary, Inc., and they tested me on

personality," Jane replied, grabbing a pair of stockings and casting around for her garter belt.

"Oh," her red-haired roommate replied, shifting her weight from one foot to another in an attempt to distract the pain. "Anything you want to talk about?"

"I would, Em, you know that," Jane said, "but I've got to get dressed. Where the hell is my pink bra?"

"So you can dress and talk at the same time?" Emma said, wishing to hell Perry's schlong were sticking up her friend's ass right about now.

Jane held her stockings in her hand and thought a moment. Perhaps she was being too secretive. After all, this was her best friend. The two of them had shared rent broken steam pipes, roaches, towel sets, boyfriends, and, possibly, Mr. Perry, if they ever fell into rent arrears again. That battery of tests that Vicky West had given her yesterday was mysterious. Perhaps sharing it with her best friend might help her understand it better.

"I... I'm not sure where to begin," Jane said, shaking her head. "You know how desperate I am for a job. And this one pays plenty. I mean more money than I've ever made before."

"Sounds good, Jane," Emma said, getting down on all fours to get comfortable so she could listen to her roommate's tale.

"I know. And Miss West is a really nice lady. A little strange, okay."

"How strange?"

"For one thing, she looks like Vampira on downers."

"You said she was beautiful."

"She is, Em. She's also mysterious. And another thing."

"Huh?" the roommate replied, getting more intrigued by the moment.

"She's got a walk-in closet in the office."

"Office supplies?"

"Not exactly."

"What then," the red-haired girl was growing impatient with her recalcitrant addle-brained roommate.

"Clothes, lots of them. And equipment. English horseback riding equipment. Some jousting stuff too, like from the Middle Ages. And masks. Some stuff you can attach to bedposts. Boots, chains, chastity belts. And whips, Em, lots of whips."

"What?" her friend replied, totally forgetting her pained ass-hole problem and coming to a thud down onto the floor. "Ouch!" she cried and bounced back up again.

"I better go now, or I'll be late for…" Jane tried to get up but felt her whole frame forced back down onto the bed. When she looked up, she saw her roommate bearing down hard on her with all the strength in her arms and legs.

"Are you nuts?" she shouted into her face. "Don't you know what's going on there?"

"No," Jane said simply, "and I figure if I just keep my nose clean and don't ask any questions…"

"My God, Jane," Emma said, spitting her words along with a generous spray of saliva, "you can't ignore what's happening."

"I am desperate," Jane said, trying to hurl her friend off her and down onto the floor. "Don't you know that? I haven't held a job for more than three and a half days in the two years since I graduated from St. Giles. I am a persona non-grata of the office world, the Typhoid Mary of the water cooler set, the most unwanted, unwelcome, blackballed, unlucky nincompoop secretary walking around town. I have been looking for a job for so long. I have been pounding the pavement till my pumps look like shredded wheat. Now let me up, and let me go to work before I bite you in the neck!"

Emma let go of her grasp and stood up slowly.

She looked sadly down at her friend whose hair she had messed up and whose tan skirt she had wrinkled badly.

"I'm sorry, Jane," she said, feeling sheepish. "I just don't want to see you get hurt."

"I don't think I'm going to get hurt," Jane said, sitting up and swinging her feet down to the carpet. "I think maybe the customer is going to get hurt. Follow?" Emma nodded her head, even though she didn't like the way it felt. She stood back and made room for her friend to pass by her.

Jane straightened her hair and checked herself in the mirror on the way out.

"One thing," Emma said, following her friend to the door, "you've got to tell me where you're going to be. Every minute. Promise?"

"Don't be ridiculous, Mum," Jane said, reaching for the front door knob.

"I mean it, Jane," the redhead said, limping toward the door as fast as she could. "Please. Look. Just pretend we're spies or something. That you're on a special assignment. That I'm the chief, running things back at the home office. Please promise me you'll call. That way, if anything happens..."

Emma felt her voice fall off. In fact, if anything did happen, she wouldn't have the slightest idea of what to do. But knowing that her friend was somewhere, anywhere, that would help. Just knowing would help her get through her day.

"Okay, Em," the blonde said, tossing her curly hair back and stepping into the hallway, "I promise."

She shut the door slowly behind her as her roommate waved to her through the slowly disappearing crack.

She headed for the elevator and, after a short ten-minute wait, finally got lucky. She hit the pavement feeling alert and ready for action. And, she had to confess, she was slightly optimistic. It's no good playing the Pollyanna bit too hard, though. She had a pretty good idea that what she was getting into might be a little shady. But she had been such a loser at everything sunny. Nothing had come to fruition, nothing, nothing, nothing. Maybe Temporary Secretary was going to be her lucky break.

"Ah, Miss Harris," the black-haired sphinx said to her when she stepped into the office. "Ready for your first assignment?"

"I hope so," Jane said, flinging her shoulder back onto the sofa.

"Good. I like your attitude." Vicky West swiveled her chair around and stepped toward the infamous closet. She opened it a little, bent over, and picked up an innocent-looking package wrapped in brown paper and tied with ordinary string.

"This is for when you get there," the woman said, practically clicking her heels together. Then she pulled the wraparound dress she was wearing apart and let the whole thing slither to the floor. It lay there in a heap. And Miss West stood in there in the middle of the room in a shiny black kid leather corset with silver studs lined up and down it, a skimpy black leather bikini top, and a black satin garter belt with mesh stockings disappearing down into black leather stiletto heeled boots.

"And this," she said, bending down to reveal a heaving heavily-endowed bust as she picked up a long, dangling piece of leather thong in one hand and a length of curled-up rope in the other," is for right now."

"What is this?" the girl asked, blinking her sea-green eyes as fast as a strobe light.

"Our final test, Miss Harris," the woman decreed, walking toward her and staring her down in her tracks.

"I hope I can pass it," Jane said, trying to fake a little grin.

"I hope so, too," the woman said, reaching into a little drawer in the closet and pulling out an evil-looking black mask. She slipped it on over her head and adjusted it so that only her eyes could be seen peeking out from behind it.

Jane couldn't stop blinking. She felt her knees turn to jelly and give way under her. Fortunately, she was standing in front of the sofa.

"Some people find this strange," the woman said, "but I see that it is largely a matter of point of view."

Jane found herself nodding but could not seem to make contact with any other part of her body.

"What is arcane, bizarre, unthinkable, to some people, is the food of life to others. Don't you see that?"

Jane continued to nod like a ventriloquist's dummy whose neck screws had worked loose.

The woman brought her black bullwhip up over her head and gave it a loud crack. The tether end of the rein suspended momentarily in mid-air then sailed downward. Jane tried to stop nodding, or at least, nod the other way, from left to right, but nothing happened. Her body just wasn't obeying her today.

"Now you will follow my orders," the black widow said, poising her poisonous stinger high up in the air again. "You will do exactly as I say, is that understood?"

Jane kept nodding.

"First of all, I want you to stop that insane nodding." The woman was speaking like the commandant of the imperial Red Army.

Jane nodded in agreement.

"I mean it." The haughty lady struck her hand down again, and a loud leather report echoed throughout the room.

Jane established contact with her neck muscles somehow and froze them in place. She could see the woman advancing toward her and holding the rope out like a lasso. Then she whirled it around her head and threw it in Jane's direction. It came down around her shoulders like a gunny sack. She felt the rope bite into her flesh as Vicky tightened it. She wondered if she was going to be branded or just led to slaughter.

"Do as I say, following my instructions to the letter," the harsh voice pierced the room, and Jane tried not to start nodding again.

"Take off your shoes," she hissed, holding tightly onto the end of the rope.

Jane reached down blindly and slipped off her navy blue pumps.

"Now, the skirt," the woman ordered.

Jane unzipped her skirt like a zombie and wiggled her hips hard to get it down without splitting it.

"The blouse," the woman said in dead, earnest tones.

Jane fought the rope helplessly as she tried to get her blouse off. Then she felt Vicky's long-fingernailed hand interrupt her fumbling. It ripped her top right off her and sent it to the floor in shreds. She sat on the sofa and resisted a shiver as she stared down at her tiny bikini panties over her blue garter belt. Her pink bra, the one that made her tits look like two tight loaves of pumpernickel fresh out of the oven, looked so innocent and helpless under the bite of the tight rope.

"Lie down," the woman commanded as she yanked the rope in such a direction as to force her down onto the sofa.

Jane felt her body smash against the furniture as her head narrowly missed the opposite arm of the sofa. She had just never been so scared in her whole life.

"What do you..." she tried in short, heaving gasps.

"Silent, Wench!" the woman screeched at her. "You will speak only when you are addressed. I will speak for both of us. Do as I command."

Jane closed her eyes on that one and felt the lids burning. She had begun to shake hard and couldn't seem to stop doing that now.

"Onto your stomach," the black cowgirl said between clenched teeth.

Jane rolled over and bit the upholstery with her chattering teeth. It tasted like the dirt of her own grave.

The black-clad mistress brought the free end of the rope around the back of the sofa and pushed it through to the front, aiming underneath it. She brought it right round and made a secure knot that rested its bulk in Jane's ass crevice. Then she brought the free end of it up and tied Jane's wrists to each other and then to the wrought iron legs of the massive piece of furniture. She threaded it under the full length of the sofa and then tied the girl's legs in a similar fashion. The whole effect made Jane feel like she was part of the furniture.

"Please don't..." She was interrupted by a gag.

Vicky was shoving something into her mouth and choking her air off with it as she tied part of it behind her head. It smelled vaguely familiar. She looked down to see the familiar cream color of her best blouse, the one the woman had shredded into pieces when she ripped the thing off her moments earlier.

The rest of her pleas came out as muffled cries and whispers.

Vicky watched as the girl thrashed her head up and down and from side to side and tried to move as the knots bit into her flesh, and the rope made it impossible for her to do much except wiggle like a worm on the end of a hook.

"Now, my proud beauty," she said, slapping her whip through the air again, "we'll see who's the mistress and who's the slave in this little ensemble."

Jane wondered why she had to say that. From the way things stood, it seemed perfectly clear to her. When you are in command of someone, when you are completely dominant over them," the woman said in a voice that sounded like rain on tinfoil, "you will understand."

Jane thought it sounded intriguing, but right now, she just couldn't get into it.

"Such lovely buttocks," the woman said, playing the tether end of her whip over them and letting it slack into the valley between her butt cheeks, "such tight, round high rises of marzipan. Good enough to take a bite out of or to make a slight indentation on. A memorable indentation."

Jane heard the whip crack up into the air before it came down with a snarl and sliced into her backside.

"Arh," she moaned as the leather thong gripped her flesh. The thing hurt, the thing really stung, but somehow, somewhere deep inside her, a tantalizing little gurgle was beginning to bubble up. Just an air pocket, but it was there. This was intriguing; she had to admit, it was different. A hell of a lot different from a timed typing test, that was for sure.

"Again, my pretty, pretty, pretty," the woman brayed as she forked the rein into the air and cut down onto the luscious melon rounds of the girl's delicate, innocent skin.

"I know, my sweet," the woman said, her confidence rising in her chest, "I know that once you sense the powerful sting of my whip, you will come to love it as much as I."

Again, the woman wasn't making much sense, but Jane wasn't feeling much sense, either. Why the hell was she feeling so damned hot, and not just down there where the woman was raising welts, either.

Vicky brought the leather thong into play once more and seized the dead, still air by force with it as she nailed it to the heaving white thighs of the girl's behind. How she loved the sound that thing made. How she loved the total feeling of power that long, stringy whip gave her. How she loved to dominate sweet young things like this completely.

And how excited she was getting, just standing here watching the girl's butt mounds rise and fall like the waves. It wouldn't be too much longer before she would have to do something about it. Before, she would have to take charge, take even more charge. Her clit was pounding against her cunt lips like sticks against a snare drum.

"Take that whip," she screamed, flailing the thing high up above her head and flogging the girl good with it. "Take it harder, you little snipe."

Jane felt her ass cheeks groan with pain, and her cunt lips begin to wail with pleasure. Such mixed feelings were welling up inside her. She didn't know whether to shout or sing. To laugh or cry.

Vicky reached around to the back pocket of her corset and produced a long, sleek, hard rubber dildo. The thing was black and had a double-head attachment so that two could ride as cheaply as one on it.

Jane was growing increasingly annoyed at herself for feeling so incredibly hot under the butt cheeks. Why was she feeling this way? After all, she was getting a spanking. And she hadn't even done anything wrong! But there it was, nevertheless, an engorged clit. And engorged clits, in Jane's experience, never lied.

Vicky whirled the wicked rubber dildo around in between her fingers like a baton at a parade. She advanced toward the prone girl and stood above her, her whip thong dangling in her hand, playing around in the sensitive crevice between the blonde girl's butt cheeks.

"Enough of the sting of my whip, Slave!" she said, bringing

the dildo close to her ass opening, "And a little of the sting of something else."

With that, she ripped the girl's panties off her ass and plugged her cunt with it.

"Agh," Jane tried to tell her again. The thing felt so evil sticking inside of her like that. So vile, so deadly, so completely destroying. Her cunt lips parted to receive it eagerly. She felt herself gurgling up harder now. To an even bubbly surface, like an active tar pit.

Vicky released her own black panties from over her garter belt and let them fall to the floor. She stepped out of them hurriedly and jumped on top of the helpless girl.

Jane felt the full weight of the woman bounce down on top of her. The dildo was plucking hard at her cunt lips, playing them like the tough strings of a steel guitar. She could feel the wetness, the sweet moisture creep over it and bathe it in steamy liquid. Her gurgling had become a monstrous groundswell. She began undulating her hips to get more pleasure from the huge rubber prick thrust inside her.

"Yes, my proud little princess," the woman said, in a loud whisper between her teeth, "fuck that thing, fuck it."

Vicky found the other end of the long, stiff dildo thing and rose up on her knees to better guide it onto her cunt lips. She chased after it with those hot, quivering, eager cunt lips of hers and played them down on it whenever she could. She made a game out of trying to entrap it between her cunt lips as she held them apart, trying to find the perfect moment to come right down onto it.

"Oh, God," the woman shrieked, "that's good." She had

just found the peak of the throbbing rubber hard-on and was making her way down the shaft. Her cunt lips gripped it with their steely locking muscles as she moved down and then, pressing her knees onto either side of the tied-up girl rose back up off it.

Jane could feel the extra pressure inside her cunt as the woman jacked herself up and down the dildo pole. It pressed hard down inside her and made her wince with pain and pleasure each time it struck. She could feel the woman's big, thick throbbing cunt lips on her own swollen red whip tracks each time she came all the way down the now-moist and glistening shaft. She was shoving the thing in and out ever deeper down inside of her. She was fucking her with that hard, bumpy dildo cock. That sensation and the one coming from those raised welts was enough to turn her groundswell into a trembling, sizzling earthquake.

"Fuck me," the woman shouted, grabbing her whip and holding onto either end of it with both hands.

She brought it down around Jane's head and over her face, then stretched it against her neck. She pulled on it hard, bringing Jane's head all the way up from the pressure against her throat.

Jane found these sensations tremendously confusing, but they did not stop the quickly increasing senses of arousal and excitation. She was being whipped, hogtied, and now choked, yet her cunt was wailing like a wounded sea lion.

Vicky pounded her whole frame harder down onto the sofa. She felt the bobbing fuck pole sticking high up into her dripping pussy hole. It stuck there like a fat man in a teeny-weeny manhole. She worked it like a madwoman up and down, around and around. The thing was actually getting hotter from so

Vicky felt herself being plugged and pounded again and again by the angry, savage dildo sticking out from between the girl's legs. She rode it as hard as a night jockey as she pulled harder and harder on the reins around Jane's neck.

"Come on, Horsie," she shouted into the girl's ear, "Come on, Horsie, ride me."

Jane bounced her hips up still harder as the penetrating pole sunk down into her wet, hot throbbing pussy place. The sound of wet slurpy slapping it made as Vicky's cunt slammed down onto her buttocks, splitting her eardrums with loud vibratos. She thrust her hips up as high as she possibly could, feeling the rope cut into her eager, hot flesh.

"Fuck me, Horsie," the woman continued, slamming the dildo cock up into her cunt and pressing down on the girl's undulating ass mounds. "Fuck, Horsie, fuck."

Jane felt a jolt of electricity strike something hard down inside her gut, and then, as though she was being immersed in warm bath water, she let go a moment and came in furious tossing and pitching waves of thundering climax. Again and again and again. And still, she wanted more. She kept the pace up as she thrust her hips up high and brought them down hard again against the flat, smooth sofa bed.

Vicky cried and moaned as she gripped the reins hard as she plunged the cock dildo up into her cunt with her ever-faster and ever-more eager riding strokes. She plugged and pumped herself with the cock hard-on. She fucked the stiff dildo in and out as fast as her short, gyrating movements would keep pace. She felt herself surge up and slam down in a blinding, ripping, snorting storm of orgiastic rushes. She came so hard she wrenched her body right off the rubber prick and had to scramble back up on it for a second round of heaving, exasperating come.

"Ahh," she cried as she passed the finish line, "nice ride, Horsie."

After a few seconds of slowed breathing and wiping the sweat off her, Vicky dismounted her pet's lovely rear end and patted the flank firmly. "Good girl." Then she strolled casually around to the head of her beast and took the gag out of Jane's mouth.

"Oh, shit!" the anxious, overwrought girl said, expelling the last of her orgiastic joy juice onto the sofa. "Did I pass, Miss West? Did I pass that one?"

"Little Vixen," the woman said, releasing the rope from around her wrists and ankles, "You did rather well, in fact."

A few moments later, Jane sat up and rubbed her butt. She was beginning to get an idea of what Emma felt like earlier today.

Vicky returned her dominance gear to the closet and tied her wraparound dress neatly in place.

"Well, Miss Harris," she said, sounding like her old officious self, I believe you are indeed ready for your first assignment. Here's the address."

"Good," Jane said, feeling quite pleased that she had passed something today besides a lot of come juice out of her cunt, "but how about the way I look?"

Jane and Miss West stared down at the ripped bra and shredded panties the girl had on. She looked like a war-torn and ravaged victim of a blitz.

"Not to worry," the woman said, reassuring her and crossing to her closet. "Here." She tossed her a pale blue wraparound dress, not unlike the modest, innocent one she was wearing. "But remember, the men at the shoe buyer's convention don't usually pay much attention to what you wear on your body. They pay more attention to what you have on your feet."

She tossed her two thick leather platform shoes with silver ankle straps that wound around up to mid-calf.

"You know how shoe salesmen are," Vicky said, standing in front of the closet like a harried housewife. She closed the doors silently and came back to where Jane was seated in her nylon and lace smithereens.

The girl smiled wanly and reached down to grab the brown paper package. She didn't know how shoe salesmen were, really, but she had a feeling she was going to find out. Soon.

6 – Strands of Pink

"I mean it, Em," the innocent voice came over the phone, "I can't talk too long either. It's a wonderful hotel. The Washington. I don't exactly know where the convention is going to be held. Something called the Starlight Room. A lot of big executives from the ladies' shoe business. That's all I know, believe me."

"Just be sure you call me in an hour," the red-haired girl said back to her, holding the phone to her ear as she leaned on her typewriter.

"Oh, Emma," Jane started to protest.

"If you don't, I'll worry myself sick." She replied, wondering what trouble her taffy-headed roommate could get into considering the circumstances.

The girls signed off and hung up. Emma went back to typing about four words an hour. She shook her head as she looked at the mumbo-jumbo on the paper. How had Jane gotten herself mixed up in this crazy scene, anyway?

She thought a few more minutes, then stopped abruptly and yanked the paper out of the machine. Then, she bolted up, grabbed her purse, flicked out the light, and headed for the front door.

Jane Harris headed down the air-conditioned corridor with the brown package strings tucked neatly between her middle two fingers. She searched for a sign that might read, "Shoe Buyers' Convention," but so far, nothing.

She found an elevator full of black men in red fezzes with miniature scimitars on their lapels. She got on and smiled like a tourist as the elevator door shut like Ali Baba's cave.

"Open Sesame," she said with a radiant smile as the elevator hit the second floor. The black men stared at her in frozen silence.

She figured the second floor, a long labyrinth of corridors and convention rooms, was probably her best bet. She looked for the door marked "Starlight Room" or "Shoe Buyers" or something similar. All the big convention rooms were either locked or full or had unfamiliar signs posted on little sandwich boards in front of them.

She continued her search. Finally, she spotted someone in a red uniform with a cap who looked like he might work in the hotel.

"Excuse me, Sir," she said politely, "could you direct me to the Starlight Room. I'm looking for the Shoe Buyers' Convention."

The uniformed man gave her a quick wink and a light elbowing in the ribs.

"Sure thing, Toots," he said, nodding and winking like a signal light. "Just go down that corridor and turn left when you reach the end."

Jane said a fond adieu, and she headed off. The man shouted after her in a loud stage whisper, "Enjoy yourself, Honey Buns."

Then she heard him let out a string of loud guffaws that followed her to the end of the hall.

She turned left like he told her to, but no rooms existed.

Only a door that said, "Fire Exit." She felt a little queer pushing on it. But it was her only real choice. It opened easily enough.

Once through it, the surroundings changed a little. The hall carpet, which had been lush and bright red, turned into a thin strip of black tuft. The lighting had been dim before, but now it was dim and red, emanating from little steel torches bolted into the walls. Other than that light, the place was pretty darn gloomy.

Jane made her way along the hall, looking for any sign of a door. Finally, she made out one at the opposite end. A small, hand-painted index card had been thumb-tacked to the door wood. And it read, "Shoe Buyers."

This must be the place, she said to herself as she took a big breath and placed her hand on the doorknob. It twisted quickly in her hand, and she pushed on the door until it opened up.

She smiled with relief when she saw the sparsely familiar reception room. It was as ordinary as any room she had been in over her secretarial career years. Upright sofa, coffee table full of last year's magazines. Long receptionist's desk with a bunch of different colored phones. And a rather average-looking girl sitting behind the desk.

"Name?" the girl said routinely.

"Jane," she smiled broadly, adding, "from Temporary Secretary."

"Ah," she said, picking up a pencil and a visitor's card pin with a little white label attached. "Yes."

Jane watched as she scribbled a few words onto the card.

Then she looked up at her through her bifocals and asked, ”Mistress or Slave?”

”Huh?” she said back.

”I asked you,” the girl said, striking a sudden attitude of assertiveness that Jane found totally unnecessary, ”if you were attending the convention as a Mistress or a Slave.”

”Oh,” Jane said, feeling her arms grow limp as cooked spaghetti.

”Which is it?” the girl snapped. Boy, she sure had changed her tune at the last minute. ”As you can see,” she continued, ”I have to fill in your card, so let’s have it.”

”Well,” Jane began slowly, ”I don’t know, you see... How do I tell? I mean...”

Before she could finish, the girl was poking her in the arm with the visitor’s card pin. Jane looked down to see it completely filled out. The word ”Slave” had been inked in over the whole thing.

”Next room,” the girl pointed blatantly, ”and I’ll take that.” Now, she was pointing to Jane’s brown package.

Jane gave it to her in a daze and then turned to follow the end of her finger toward the door on her left.

She marched intently toward it. Little office snit! She’d seen them before. They were in every single office she had ever set foot in. How come people couldn’t just be friendly, she wondered. Give somebody a desk and a couple of telephones, and... Wow!

Jane’s thoughts were broken off by an ear-piercing scream that split her attention in two the moment she walked into the room. Then the sights took over, and she had to brace herself against the door behind her to take them all in.

The room was about the size of a regular school classroom. But there, the resemblance ended – except for the punishment. There was a lot of it going on in the room. In every corner, in fact. Women were tied to stakes with their rear ends exposed. Women were gagged with harnesses around their necks strung up between hooks in the ceiling, from which a few dangled in face-to-crotch positions. Some were dressed in black leather outfits, much like the one Vicky West had on earlier that day. Women stood with bullwhips, some with riding crops, administering punishment. Men were being led around the room on leashes like dogs. Black leather, chains, crops, handcuffs, leather belts, snapping, cracking, popping, red welts, screams of pain, others screaming as they inflicted it. These were the sights and sounds that assaulted her senses. These were the scenes of a dungeon.

As far as Jane could tell, the only thing missing was a torture rack. One bare-chested, powerfully built man stepped toward her. She had no idea who he was, as he was wearing a black executioner's hood over his face. He wore black leather breeches and carried a leather slave whip.

Jane tried to open the door again but found it locked. She pulled the hand holding the card behind her back, but the big man grabbed it from her.

She stared at him in awe and terror as he read what was so plainly marked on it.

"We've been waiting for you. Follow me," was all the man

said. He gestured toward the center of the room with his whip handle.

Jane was unsure what to do, but something told her to follow him, whatever else she had planned.

She padded along after him with mixed feelings as he led the way with wide, aggressive boot stomps.

"A slave, Mistress," he said, bowing to a huge, statuesque silver-haired woman decked out in tight leather pants with a halter top made of studded leather pierced with holes so abundant that it looked like a heavy fishnet. Only the nipples of her breasts were hidden by huge steel tips in the shape of nipples. She was wearing the highest-heeled boots Jane had ever seen. She couldn't even figure out how she could walk on them.

"Down on your knees," the woman commanded. She held the biggest, thickest, meanest leather lash Jane could imagine. It had five separate thongs dangling off one end. She must be a whip specialist just to operate it.

Again, the woman ordered her, "Get down, Slave!" When Jane stared back at her, she pushed her down to the ground with the heel of her boot.

Jane stared up at the woman who looked about the size of the Statue of Liberty from her position on the floor. She might have been a gorgeous woman, or she might have been the ugliest one alive. There was no telling. She wore a mask that curved up in haughty black peaks and swirls at the temples. Only her eyes were visible.

"Now bow down to me, Scum Whore!" the woman said, asserting her whole weight on Jane's shoulder with her boot.

Jane caught on quite quickly this time. She cast her eyes downward and bent her head over far, so far she could only glimpse the toes of the woman's stacked boots.

"Now kiss my boot," the woman said in a preening, haughty voice. A voice that made the hairs on Jane's neck stand up.

"Holy Shit!" she spilled out, realizing she was in hot water. These people were not fooling around. No, Sireee!

"Wretched Street Trash!" the woman shouted, "How dare you speak to me in that flippant tone. I'll teach you to speak right, won't we, Basil?"

The black hooded man approached her and took a position at her right side.

"As Mistress commands," he said, bowing and moving in on Jane.

She gripped the stone floor with her fingernails so hard they broke off. How the hell had she gotten into this in the first place? Better still, how the hell was she going to get out of it?

"Seize her and beat her!" the woman commanded, whirling around to give a few more male dominants the word on what they could do with this intolerable bitch.

Four or five men came rushing up from various parts of the room, and since Jane was afraid to look up, she could only spot them out of her peripheral vision.

They cuffed her by the right and left arms and then yanked her onto her feet. They half-dragged, half-hauled her to the nearest empty neck collar, shackled to the floor on a long steel chain.

Jane felt the stiff leather brace encircle her neck, pinching her skin, hair, and her pride. She felt it lock securely into place, and then she saw someone, a black hooded male, force the ring into the collar into an open hasp. When the thing clicked shut, she let out a scream. It was followed by the silver-haired Mistress's whip, which cracked like a gunshot.

"Silence, Slut!" she crowed, bringing the whip back over her head. "You are making your already untenable position all that much worse."

Jane sank onto her knees and felt the tears roll down her cheeks. She didn't know why she was crying. Nobody was hurting her, but she had a feeling it wouldn't be long now.

"Bind her!" the woman in charge shouted to her men. They obeyed instantly.

Jane felt a leather-lined wrist cuff go around her left and right wrist. They snapped shut with the finality of a jail cell closing behind a condemned man.

"Why..." she heard herself say in her whine. "Why me?"

"Shut that pink, slimy trap of yours," the she-bitch snarled, and she cracked her whip for emphasis.

Jane had to admit that with that thing in her hand, she presented a powerful picture of authority.

"Spread those legs of hers out... far out," the witch snapped, "Harder!"

Two of the men got on one side and two on the other. They spread Jane's shapely legs apart and manacled her on both sides and the ankles. She felt a little rip tear up from her ass and split to her cunt. These black-faced beefcakes were stretching her in two.

"Excuse me, but do you mind?" she stared timidly, "I think this has gone just about far..."

The bitch cracked her whip about an inch away from Jane's twitching pug nose. She said nothing more. Neither did Jane. But she heard the awful clanking of the manacles around her ankles and looked over her shoulder as best she could to see chains stretching out from her ankles and heading toward two ugly protruding meat hooks sticking up out of the stone floor.

She shriveled on the spot to think of what might come next. She looked down as best she could to see the insanely inane little wraparound dress still clinging to her body. She looked like a coed who had met with foul play on her way to cheerleading practice. Except for those slutty-looking platform shoes. They fit right into this bizarre convention.

"Who wants to be the first," the woman shouted to everyone in attendance.

Jane looked a little to her right and saw a few people sitting in chairs on one side of the room, like a peanut gallery.

"Who wants to administer the first blow of the lash?" the woman ordered.

A nicely dressed man in a three-piece suit with a black hood over his face stepped forward. Jane could barely make him out. He looked like some executive or another. He is probably here on his lunch hour. They had all begun to look pretty much alike to her by this time, whether in the office or at the auction block.

She felt the wraparound dress come ripping right off her back. She nearly died of embarrassment when she remembered that her panties and bra were ripped until she thought it was probably okay since they would end up more shredded by the time this was over. Whenever that would be.

Then she felt a mighty hand grip the back strap of her bra and tear it off her breasts and down her middle. The wind whizzed past her naked nipples, giving them a titillating breeze making her nipples stand up erect.

"All right," she said, knowing it would probably lead nowhere, "now look what you've done..."

"That's enough!" the black queen shrieked, snapping the whip onto the floor at her heels. "Gag her!"

Sure enough, someone was right there to do it. She felt a heavy harness-like thing come down over her blonde curls and cut off her vision for a moment. Then she felt a little rubbery ball, a flabby balloon tucked into her mouth. The overwhelming feeling of helplessness she felt was really starting to frighten her. There she was, her words about to be cut off, and she couldn't do a single thing about it.

She felt really out of it when that flabby ball inflated inside her mouth. Luckily, her nose holes were free. There was no way she could express herself now except to cry. She felt the tears well up in the corners of her eyes, preparing to spill out.

The shadows of the action behind her back played on the wall beside her. She could see the sordid events distorted and larger than life, playing in the flickering shadows of the stone wall. Eerie shadows bounced around there. This was a circus, all right. A freak show. And she was the center attraction.

She felt the wet tears spill out and down her cheeks. They splattered down toward her breasts and out over her nipples.

Then she ground her heels hard into the concrete floor and prepared herself for the whipping she knew would come.

"Step right up, Sir," the Iron Mistress said to the man, snapping her fingers together. A slave brought up a tray of choice punishment equipment. A mace, a riding crop, and a leather-covered paddle. Cat o' nine tails. Clothes pins, C-clamps. Other instruments of pain and torture.

"Have you made your selection?" the black bitch said imperiously.

"I have, Mistress," the man said, fitting his giant ringed fingers around a slippery leather whip handle.

"An excellent choice," the woman said, gesturing toward the helpless body of the blonde girl. "Our slave awaits her punishment."

The man gripped the slithery tip of the big bullwhip in one hand and the thick, leathery handle in the other. He advanced toward the writhing, twisting body hanging deliciously suspended from hooks.

Those delectable curvy white thighs, those high-rising buns flinching and gripping each other, that smooth, arched back, the blonde tresses, now falling in such confusion every which way over the girl's silken shoulders. He was going to enjoy whipping the shit out of her, that was for sure.

He reared up with every muscle in his body and poised for the strike. He held the sinewy leather strand in mid-air for a tantalizing moment before he snapped it hard and brought it down full force on the resisting, tossing girl's backside.

It slapped down hard, like a speed boat hitting rough water.

With the first horrible snap of the whip, the man felt his erect member clang against his pants like an errant dinner bell.

Jane felt the sting of the mean leather flail against the tender flesh. It burned like a ring of fire. The track on her back smarted and swelled up immediately as soon as the man brought the whip off her back. She winced and fought the tears that rolled down her cheeks. It felt awful, just awful, to be tied up like that. To be made to feel so helpless, so low, so subhuman. Then, before she had time to add all her thoughts up, the man struck again. And this time, the blow really hurt. He hit her right between her ass cheeks, right up into her crotch.

Jane could see one colossal male dominant come into her field of vision. The bulge in his leather breeches was so enormous she had to look away. But she couldn't help looking right back. It was poking hard against the metal teeth of his zipper, forcing it out in a wide basket arc.

But her attention was drawn elsewhere again quickly as the leather whip again gave off a loud crack before it struck the skin of her back, laying a long track along her spine red and bare.

Shit, that hurts! She said to herself, feeling as helpless as a fly in a spider web. I wonder how long he intends to keep that up. Jane turned her head momentarily against the wall to see one of the other female slaves being forced down to her knees at the foot of the man whipping her. Then, in the shadows, she could make out the form of the woman being forced toward the man's crotch. She watched in shock and surprise as the woman unzipped the man's crotch and released his erect member. Then she saw the shadow of the woman taking the man's cock into her mouth and sucking on it. But even with all that action going on, the man did not diminish his whipping, not one little bit.

She turned her attention back to the pain of her red, swollen backside. Her buttocks must have looked like Indianapolis Speedway by now. It felt like it, too. The male dominant standing guard at her side, the one with the substantial erect front, was now unzipping himself. He took a huge, long dick about the size of a Polish sausage and slowly, slowly began to masturbate.

Jane was amazed at how nonchalant he was about it. He stood there with that insanely, obscenely huge schlong of his pointing out toward the enrapt audience while Jane was getting a beating a runaway slave in deepest Georgia wouldn't have stood for.

She watched in absolute amazement as the man took his big gripping paw and covered the whole huge top of his slippery smooth cock knob with it and began to work it around slowly, like the handle of a coffee grinder, a huge coffee grinder.

"Suck his dick!" she heard someone from the audience cry out.

She was pretty sure they couldn't have meant her. They must have been cheering for the woman sucking her assailant's dick. She cast her glance once more to the side and saw in shadow the woman working her mouth up and down hard on what appeared to be the longest dick she had ever seen, but it was in shadow, and those things do tend to distort in such capricious light.

"Ooooohh," she heard the dominant stud say who was standing next to her. She drew her attention back to him and watched as he pried his meat around and around by simply gripping the head of his giant dick wand and shifting its gear.

She watched, transfixed, as the blows rained down on her back, and the man slid his monster huge hand up and down his gigantic erect prick shaft. He was working it very slowly, building up the tension, but for whose benefit, Jane wondered, as she felt herself grow somewhat aroused despite her attempts to control the sensation. She could never resist a masked man playing with his pecker meat right before her. Perhaps he was teasing her, after all.

The big black hooded stud played his hand up and down his monster meat, getting the shaft hard and wet. The thing thudded under the huge lock grip of his palm as he slid his hand up to the head, made a large circle over the tacky, moist dome, and gripped it again to begin the long trip back down. He let his hands slide down and grasp the hilt hard. He cupped one hand around his pulsating, hard rocking balls and let the other hand do the duty of sliding back up his shaft, producing more pre-cum droplets every inch. Then he spread the sticky tacky stuff down over his rock-hard shaft, now glistening in the torchlight of the room, all the way down to the base of his peter. The thing was stiffening under his hands, growing harder with each rise and fall of his muscular palms.

The hair follicles on his balls felt like nerve endings of needle-point showers as he jarred his cock a little, beginning a circular motion over his huge crown dome head. Then, he let his hands slide down back over his stiff, throbbing shaft to the hilt again and back up. He was building up a rhythm and speed that made his onlookers gasp excitedly.

Jane couldn't take her eyes off the throbbing, hard dick. As much as she could feel the pain, this distraction was a blessed relief. She could feel the smoke and steam of arousal rising up inside her. She could feel her cunt lips puffing up with the juice and engorgement of arousal. She could feel herself getting hot, and she resented it a lot. The pain, the arousal, the pain, the arousal, the arousal, the pain, the hot horny lusty, sexy, sexy way she couldn't stop, couldn't control, couldn't do anything about.

She watched in growing excitation as the man whisked his heavy hands up and down the full length of his monster pecker. She saw him glide and slide those two hands in and out of every possible position as he gripped his fuck pole and stroked, stroked, harder and harder, faster and faster. Cling and jerk, back and forth, up and down. Around and around.

He drew her into his vortex with every slippery, enticing move of throbbing hard whang.

Shit, she thought to herself. Where's the cock that should be slipped into my cunt right now? What a bummer!

The dominant hooded stud with his prick in his hand kept one eye on the bouncing big tits waving in front of him as he drew his meat up to full length in front of him and pulled his hands back down the slimy shaft, only to send it up top again, faster and faster. Her tantalizing siren's tits were waving at him, welcoming him, bringing his arousal to a hot, heavy pitch.

His arousal was building, building harder and hotter and higher with each sweep of his hand up and down, down and up the thick, hot shaft. His meat glowed wet and throbbing under his glancing handiwork. Over and over his cock, he flailed his strong fingers as he watched Jane's tits, as he saw the whipping man fling his whip into her white, throbbing flanks, as he showed the crowd his tremendous meat stick, his big, hot dick weapon. He pulled harder and harder until he felt his butt muscles tighten to the breaking point. And then… Bang! He shot out his white load. He blew his spunk all over Jane's white tits. He creamed on her pulsating flesh mounds.

Jane's eyes shot open and banged shut as the jism flew onto her wiggling, writhing tits. She felt the hot load cream down her nipples and stick to her boob mounds. The thick, creamy goo oozed over her breasts and ran toward her aching, hot cunt. She felt the trickle slide in between her cunt lips and felt the juice masturbate her cunt. It cradled and bathed her cunt in its delicious still-warm juice.

That little drop of come was all she needed. She opened her eyes in a pitch of excitation as she glanced over the wall and saw the shadow of the whipping man's prick shoot its spray load. It shot out a big, thick round of come juice that she could only see in shadow.

The juice of her cunt mingled with the man's jism juice, and the sight on the wall combined to give her a hard, hot rush of heavy, gyrating orgiastic come. She blushed purple and blue and felt the whip dig into her flesh again and again as the waves of orgasm pelted her one after another. As the blanket of pain and ecstasy covered her layer after layer.

She was not even vaguely aware that the door to the room had opened and that a young, fashionable couple had walked in. She did not see the couple approaching where she was strung up like a side of beef. She did not see or hear or feel them pointing excitedly toward her. And she was totally unaware of their conversation.

"Chloe," Lucas Keating said, pointing to the strung-up girl victim. "What about this?"

Chloe Keating took a long, astute, studied look at the voluptuous, innocent form of the slave strung up in front of her eyes. The welts on her back formed strands of pink ribbon from her shoulders to her ass cheeks. Her high hot tight butt mounds were heaving and sweating with the pain of resistance. Her upturned tits were wringing wet with the moisture of arousal, pain, and punishment. "She'll do," the woman said, sizing up the situation, "she'll do just fine."

7 – The suite

Jane didn't remember much about being taken out of the shackles that had made her ankles and wrists so swollen and sore. She had very little recollection of the Keating couple wrapping her in a fur coat and paying an enormous sum of money to the headmistress for her.

She did remember bobbing and weaving in the middle of the room. Feeling still hot and bothered, aroused, slightly bemused, very abused. And hurt. God, was she hurting.

"Where are you taking me?" she asked as the couple escorted her out. Again, the beige and brown tones of the reception room glanced past her. She felt as if she were on a roller coaster. A roller coaster going up and down but leading nowhere, nowhere she wanted to go.

"We've taken a little suite, just for the occasion," the tall, reddish-blonde woman said. They both edged her out the door and down the long corridor. Had someone drugged her? The hall was pitching and rolling like a ship on a storm-tossed sea. And she was seized with a bout of nausea to accompany the bad trip.

"I think, I think I'm gonna throw…" She broke away from the man's grasp a moment and felt herself heave up and over the side rails as she tossed her vomit onto the fire extinguisher perched on one side of the hall.

"This is a sick girl," Lucas Keating said, wondering why they had picked her. But as the fur coat slipped off her back and he glimpsed the gorgeous drop-dead delectable figure on the little slave, he nodded in understanding.

The funny thing was that she looked a little like his wife. The same coloring. Though his wife's hair was reddish and straighter. They were both willowy. And stacked. Then, they both turned him on just looking at those voluptuous tits of the girl's and thinking about the big, stiff upturned ones his wife had.

"Let's get her to the rooms right away," Chloe said, grabbing her around the wrist and guiding her toward the "Fire Exit' door.

Somehow, the three of them made their way out of it. They sped down the hotel hallway toward the elevator. The vista looked familiar to Jane, but she couldn't quite place it in her vague, dazed awareness.

However, when the elevator opened, some of it returned to her. There were those black men again, with the red fezzes, bobbing and grinning at each other. Until she got on. Then they stiffened up and stared blankly ahead. The whole scene made Jane think she was in a marketplace in Marakesh or Tangiers. The black men were slave traders, and the couple gripping her wrists were white slave kidnappers. She was going to be taken to some mysterious port of call and forced to live with a eunuch in a harem or some other despicable Asian fate.

"Help," she tried to speak through parched, dried lips, "I don't want to live in a harem."

Again, the stony passengers of the elevator ignored her outburst.

The elevator chugged up to the fourteenth floor and opened as Jane felt herself being nudged off. She tried to wave a limp goodbye to the black men, the last humans she was afraid she would ever again see on this earth before she was banished to the interior of a sheik's palace. How sad, how romantic, how painful. And speaking of pain, those welts on her back were starting to have their way with her.

"Owww," she said as the couple, and she made their way down the hall.

"We'll have to do something about those bruises," the woman said quite calmly, "right away."

Jane was aware that they weren't moving anymore. She watched impassively as the man turned the key in the lock and pushed the door open. He kicked at it with his foot as he caught her just before she slid to the floor.

Suddenly, the three of them were inside, and someone was running the shower. She heard ice being poured out of an ice bucket. Hell of a time for a drink, she thought to herself. Then, she felt the ice, now wrapped in a cool terry cloth towel, being applied to her head. Another pack was slapped on her back.

A few moments later, she knew she was standing under a cool shower. And then she was being dried off. Very thoroughly, too. She could hear giggling and talking. Someone even started stroking her breasts, not bad if she had been in the mood. She wasn't at that particular moment.

"Let's get her to bed," the woman's voice said. "Then let's slip this down her."

Jane wondered what the hell they were going to slip down her, but she could not do so much as ask.

She felt a pair of smooth, massaging hands rub a balm onto her welts, and some pain disappeared.

"Here," a male voice said, "drink this."

She felt her head held up, and a glass of liquid came to her lips. She drank eagerly, only dimly aware that the liquid had a sweet, sticky undertaste. She lay her head back on the pillow or something soft and felt herself nod, nod, nod off into a deep, dreamless sleep.

When she woke up, she felt alert and a whole lot clearer. She blinked and stared up at the ceiling. Now, if she could just remember who she was and how she got here, everything would fall naturally into place. She was sure.

"Welcome back to the world of the living," a satiny, smooth voice said reassuringly.

"Oh," Jane said, hopefully, "It's good to be alive."

"I agree," the dark, curly-haired man with the build like Apollo said to her.

"By the way," she said, batting her eyes and fluffing her hair, "who are you?"

A long pause. Then, the honey voice of the sexy woman came to play like a zither in her ears. "You can think of us as, well, as your captors."

"What?" Jane said, sitting up in bed and feeling for the covers, which were nowhere to be found.

"Relax," the barrel-chested man said, "perhaps that word frightens you. And we wouldn't want you to be. At least, not yet."

Jane stared at the pair in horror. What were these two doing here anyway? They were dressed beautifully. That was evident. The woman was wearing a long black gown with a very revealing dip in the front. The man wore a smoking jacket and a pair of black satin pants. They looked like they were about to have brunch on the terrace. Only there was no terrace, and it wasn't time for brunch.

"What do you want from me?" she said with those big, green, innocent eyes that invariably got her into hot water. "What am I doing here?"

"Just exactly what you're doing," the man said, smiling a sexy smile out of the corner of his mouth. He looked like Rhett Butler.

"I'm sitting in a strange room with two strange people, and I don't mind telling both of you I feel strange about it," Jane countered, wondering if that argument made any sense whatsoever.

"You're pleasing us by your presence," the woman crooned, "Can that be bad?"

"I don't know," Jane said, wishing she had more on than a flimsy towel wrapped around her like a sarong, "I've stopped thinking in terms of good and bad ever since this morning."

"Like us," the man said, pacing the floor at the foot of her wide, brass bed. "We've also stopped thinking in terms of good and bad. You see, we, my wife and I, that is, we have come to believe only in the states of pain and pleasure. We make no value judgments about either of them. As far as we are concerned, good and bad are matters of personal choice."

Jane thought hard about that one for a moment. And she didn't like it one bit.

"Does the phrase consenting adult mean anything to you?"

she asked, with one eye on her peek-a-boo terry cloth sarong. It seemed to be slipping off of her. "Or how about the word kidnapping. Do you like that one? Maybe the term federal offense?"

She realized that her sarong was not slipping at all. It was being pulled off. Pulled off her battered and abused gorgeous little body. Yanked right down over her popping big tits and silky pussy mound. By the woman sitting right there beside her.

"You are tasty," the woman said, raising her hand and pinching one of Jane's rosy round nipples. "I'd like to play with you."

"I don't think you want to play," Jane said, feeling her nipple respond despite her attempts to discourage it. It bobbed up like a life buoy in troubled waters. Hard and bouncing. "I think you have something else in mind."

"Don't be too cynical," the man said, "just because you've been through a rough patch."

"Rough patch?" the girl said incredulously, "I've just been beaten to within an inch of my life. And you call that a rough patch?'

"The question," the woman said now, prowling her hand toward Jane's other succulent big nipple, "is not whether you were beaten or not but if you enjoyed it."

Jane bit her bottom lip and wished she could button it there. She thought hard before she responded.

"Yes and no," she said, feeling a little creamy in her jeans. The woman was getting her more than a little aroused with her insistent fondling.”On the one hand, it hurt like hell. And I won’t deny it. On the other, it was sort of...”

”Kinky?” the man interrupted her.

”Yeah,” she said, nodding and feeling her nipples harden like clay in a kiln. ”How did you know?”

”Because I’ve been there, Sweetheart,” the man said, standing up and pulling his robe off.

Jane caught a glimpse of his he-man chest before he turned around so that she could see the welt scars on his back. They looked so cruel and heartless. Also, they looked intriguing.

”Oh,” she said, feeling the woman’s hand slither down toward the crack between her legs.

”You’ve gotten a little bruised down here,” the woman purred, ”I’m going to rub some salve in. It won’t hurt.”

Sure enough. She reached for a tan jar of something or other and scooped up a gob of it onto her fingers. Then she proceeded to ply Jane’s crack with the most elegant, smotheringly suggestible hand movements. Her little fingers were everywhere. Covering and fondling and probing and circling. Her cunt lips felt like they were being kissed by a herd of butterflies.

Jane felt a tinge of embarrassment as she realized her cunt lips were clacking together again. They always insisted on doing this at the slightest provocation. And right now, they sounded like a freight train on a loose track.

She wasn’t sure, but it felt like the man’s hands had joined the woman’s. One person couldn’t possibly be touching her in all those places at once. She felt herself melt like a weeping candle. She was so ready, so completely ready to give herself to the care of these two, and it felt so damn good to have two such adept people working on you, bringing your cunt lips together and out, together and out. Getting your clitoris worked up like a steam shovel.

"Oh, God," she heard herself say as she slumped down onto the bed. "Would one of you like to fuck me?"

She opened her eyes immediately as soon as she felt the absence of that delicious stroking. There was no one plying her cunt lips together or pinching her nipples. She looked up to see the man slipping out of his silky pajama bottoms. She saw his schlong dangling between his tree trunk thighs. She blinked in disbelief. At least, maybe he was going to fuck her. That would feel good just about now.

She could see the woman on the other side of the next bed slipping out of her gown. Her tits looked like two snow-covered ski jumps with red flags waving atop them. She had the most lustrous strawberry blonde bush and the straightest, creamiest legs. Curvy in all the right places.

Christ, Jane thought to herself. Maybe they're both going to fuck me. Okay. I guess I'm up for it.

Then she watched as the man slipped into a black leather jock strap with an ugly steel zipper mounted on the front. He tucked his enormous whang inside and zipped the thing up with a huge, steel roar.

The woman was getting into her own set of black leathers. A whale-boned corset with grommets in the front and laces that she had to pull in tight and tie off. The thing looked like leather and clung to her like it was.

She reached down and retrieved a black bikini bra from

the bed. She could barely stuff her gigantic tits into it, but after a struggle, she snapped it up in the back. Then she sat down and eased her legs and calves and thighs and stunning white hips into a tight little leather garter belt with long free-swinging garter. She reached over and grabbed a pair of web-meshed stockings and began to stretch them over her toes, then tantalizingly inch by inch up her legs.

Jane knew the man was binding his waist with a huge leather cinch belt. Gigantic steel loops hung from it. Then she noticed that one of those steel loops wasn't empty. A thick English riding crop was stuck in it.

The woman stuck her leg up high and pulled a skin-tight leather boot with crisscross steel stays on it onto her foot. Then she zipped it up. The heel was about as thick as a mattress. She repeated the procedure on her other foot.

Jane sighed and wished her cunt wasn't as wet as it was. Then she saw the woman stand up, take a mask off the nightstand, and put it on her face. Her lovely features disappeared, and in their place, a mean-looking black leather mask adorned with silver sequins.

The man grabbed a similar mask without the sequins and popped it on over his handsome features.

Then, the two of them advanced toward Jane as she cowered in bed.

"Follow us, Slave," the woman commanded, "do our bidding as we order you to, and you will survive this ordeal. But if you cross us or attempt to defy us in any way, we will be forced to retaliate mercilessly. Do you understand?"

Jane nodded her head meekly.

She felt the man's knee thrust up into her groin. And that hurt!

"Address your mistress as 'Mistress', Slave!" the man roared.

Again, the wave of hopelessness hit Jane square in the face. These people meant what they said. And she didn't want to try to defy them in case they didn't.

"Sit," the man said, going over to a swivel chair at the enormous hotel room desk and twirling it toward her.

Jane wished she had something more to put on her rear end. Or something to cover her breasts or her open, exposed pussy, but she was fresh out of luck. She held her head down and made for the chair. She climbed up on it and felt the brisk stiff leather seat intrude on the soft white sanctity of her ass cheeks.

"Kiss my boot," the woman shot down from her lofty heights. She was standing on eight-inch heels, which made her dizzy with power.

Jane sat with her head bowed as the woman brought her leathered foot up sharply and stuck it right in her face.

"Lick it, Slave!" the man coaxed as he elbowed her with the brunt end of his riding crop.

She had to admit they both presented a powerful argument for doing precisely as they commanded.

She stuck her throbbing, hot pink tongue out and let it swoop down over the leather toe. She made contact with the smooth, black, shiny leather with her wet, pulsating tickler tongue. The connection was electric.

Jane felt her tongue go soft at once and begin to slobber and slaver all over the woman's big boot tip. The leather was exquisite to the taste and touch. It was so brutal, so forced, so inexplicably exciting. She was totally in their power, totally wed under their thumb. They could do with her whatever they wished, and she would have to obey. She felt her eyes snap shut as she licked fervently. She could only hope they would be good to her. She was getting extremely excited doing this.

The man looked down at the girl's shapely backside as she licked and slurped his wife's boot. The sight of that girl humbling herself before the iron hand of his power-crazed wife made him instantly hard. He could not control himself. Seeing that blonde hair flowing onto his wife's harsh boot made him unbelievably stiff, throbbing, pulsating, and huge. He could feel his cock thrashing against the metal zipper case. It was demanding to be set free.

Chloe Keating could feel the arousal rising and falling in her big, heaving tits. She could feel it well up inside her cunt, too, thickening her lips and making them weep with anticipation. The sight of this slender, voluptuous, helpless young girl leaning down and humbling herself in front of her made her heady with power and desire.

"I think this slave is a born sucker!" she said, drawing her boot away from the eager girl's mouth. "Let's give her something more challenging to suck on."

She snapped her fingers and ordered her dominant over to her side. She pointed to his throbbing leather basket.

He straddled the girl's narrow white thighs and lifted his hips so hard he stuck the black pouch right in her face. It was hot and swelling up hotter every second.

"Now," the woman snarled. "Open that zipper with your teeth!"

Jane felt shame and degradation burn onto her cheeks and forehead. How dare these two ask her to do such a low thing. It was unthinkable. She shook her head back and forth a few times, defying them.

"You dare to defy me?" the blonde temptress recoiled. "Never!"

She snapped her fingers, and Jane felt a huge, stiff neck bracelet encircle her tiny neck. It clanked shut and held her head so rigidly in place she feared her neck would snap if she moved in either direction. Then she felt her head pulled back, probably by a leash hooked onto the neck cuff. They must have anchored it somewhere because she couldn't move her head. Terror gripped her. Fear covered her like the night, and she began to shake.

"Again, I command you, Slave," the woman said, bringing that big, thick riding crop down over her head so she could see it. "Unzip your Master's pants with your teeth."

Jane blocked out the pain around her neck by closing her eyes and trying to forget about it for a moment. No good. And besides that, the smell and feel of hot leather was blistering her lips.

She must have hesitated a moment too long. She felt the familiar gripping against her wrists. The man was putting manacles on her. She looked to see them snap shut, but no. It was a rope. She was being tied up, right into that chair, like a martyr to a stake.

"Oh, no," she cried out, "please."

"Do as we say, Slut," the woman crowed, "or worse will happen to you."

Jane swallowed hard and stretched her neck as far as the iron brace would allow her. She bared her teeth toward the silver steel zipper tab and opened her mouth wide. She brought her mouth down on the steel protuberance and gripped it hard. Then she began to tug at it with all the muscles in her mouth. It came down stiffly and with great difficulty, but still, she gripped and tugged and pursued it as far as it would go. The hot, hard bundle inside didn't make things any easier.

"Now, work his meat out with your tongue, Vile Wench!" the woman snapped, bringing the riding crop down hard onto the back of Jane's head. It felt like a guillotine blade.

Jane pried the man's huge cock out of its leather cage. It wasn't easy, either. His prick was so huge, stiff, throbbing, hard, and pulsating that it practically defied touch. Her mouth muscles ached when she released the rock-hard bundle from its hole.

"Now, Suck, Bitch!" the blonde siren wailed. "Suck his cock and do it well."

Jane leaned over a little more and paused a moment. But it was one moment too long. The woman's hard, heavy hand landed a blow to her, and the thudding sound of the riding crop came into her ears as the pain of the blow lit up her nerve endings.

"Owwww," she managed before the man stuffed his pecker inside her mouth.

Jane knew her air would be cut off if she didn't immediately begin to suck this man. This tremendous, heavy load that he plied in and out of her mouth. The dome felt like it must have been about the size of the one on the capitol building.

"Suck that load, Hopeless She-Devil!" the stormy blonde was at it again.

Chloe gripped her crop hard and ruffled the girl's tresses with it rudely. The sight of the blonde head going down on her husband's hard long dick was enough to make her melt her leathers. She felt herself oozing come cream long before climax. The sight was arousing her tremendously.

Lucas Keating felt the entwining, hot helpless lips embrace his huge, flailing cock rod. He rammed it in and out as swiftly and as hard as he possibly could. This was no time for easy foreplay. His arousal sent spurs of pain shooting down to his boots. His cock felt like a diving rod stiffening the closer it got to the water source. Harder, harder, he plunged his heaving whang down her tiny sucking hole.

More, more of the man's hopelessly huge cock was worming its way down her slithering gullet. Where was she going to put all this? He was going to poke her tonsils out. Oh, Christ, Jane thought, as her cunt lips grew ever stiffer with the inflammation of heat and desire. Where would this end? Where?

The man worked his ramrod in and out of those pouty pink lips. All the way to the head, all the way to the hilt. Hilt to head. Head to hilt. He felt the girl purse her lips hard to disallow his entrance, but still, he forced his way down inside. He looked up to see his wife's quivering pussy lips glistening before him. And he reached his whole big hairy arm down toward it.

Chloe felt her husband's giant fingers thrust right up inside her waiting, wet cunt. They circled up and around inside her, prying more joy juice loose from her pussy. The intrusion, the harsh poking, prodding hook thrust up inside her so roughly, made her seethe with pleasure and agony. She looked down to see the girl's cunt lips quivering as hers had a moment ago.

"Here, Wicked Girl!" she muttered and thrust the brunt end of her crop right between Jane's puffed-up cunt lips. Then she worked it back and forth stiffly, causing the heat of friction to do its duty on the helpless, withering girl.

Jane felt the crude leather arm buffet and plummet against her outstretched cunt lips. She stroked the man's huge flesh rod with her lips, and she fucked his giant pole with her mouth. She sweated, and she sucked, and she crammed the insanely hard, wicked tool down into her mouth and out her swollen, wet lips. She blew and sucked and tickled and licked the man's gigantic cock with every ounce of strength. She felt her cheeks suction in and out, out and in, as she continued to pull him down inside her throat. Then she let him back up again, only to swallow him another time, so far, he saw his balls disappear. Then he pulled back out a moment and held his rock-hard schlong against the tip of the girl's seething lips. The tip of his big pecker rested there a moment, a moment in time and space, suspended, suspended in the height of arousal before he shot. He shot a load of man coming out the end of his waving ramrod. He sprayed the juice all over the girl's face, down her throat, into her hair. He shot, and he sprayed. He sprayed as he shot.

"Oh, God," Jane cried out in pure agony as the hot load hit her broadside.

She felt the woman's riding crop ply itself back and forth across her raised clit knob. It worked back and forth hard enough to rub her raw. But it only succeeded in arousing her to a come pitch. She felt herself give way to the whole embracing blanket of orgasm that covered her. She let go and erupted into a torrent of squeezing hot orgasms.

"Christ," Chloe shouted as she felt the riding crop working itself at the other end of her grip. Then she felt her husband's hard hand find its mark. It pressed her button of arousal down so hard that she blasted off into space. She felt her cunt split open and the come cream run out. She felt her insides head straight up into the sky as she fought to keep her boots planted on the ground.

The sights and sounds the three of them made became a moaning, groaning trio of weird instruments, aching, reaching for a single sound. That sound came as a knock on the door of the hotel suite.

"Tap, tap, tap," it sounded.

The three of them could hardly hear it over their heavy breathing. Still, it came again: "Tap, tap, tap."

"Room service," a girl's voice announced from the other side.

The voice intruded on Chloe and Bob's concentration. It broke their arousal as they spent themselves in heaving heavy gasps of air. But the voice was familiar to Jane. It was the voice of her roommate. It was Emma's voice.

8 – A FRIEND IN NEED

"We didn't order anything from room service," the big man's healthy baritone voice rang out.

"Room service," the girl persisted.

"What the hell?" the woman shouted, ripping her mask off. "What's this about, Lucas?"

"Room service," the faceless voice shouted through the wood fibers.

"Send that little snit away," the woman said, pacing the floor worriedly.

"Special delivery," the voice said in a firm, demanding tone.

"Oh, good God," the woman said, tossing her husband his smoking jacket, "see what the hell she wants and get rid of her."

Lucas Keating slid the mask off his face and grabbed the smoking jacket. He threw it over his shoulders and did his best to tuck it around his middle. His leather breeches and black boots stuck out below it, an apparent mismatch.

The burly man strode toward the door and turned the handle. He opened the door just a crack. Jane could see absolutely nothing where she was sitting. She had her back turned away from the door, and it was a fact that was kicking her in the ass about now. She tried to crane her neck to see what was happening, but she was locked into place. Locked fast and facing front, and she couldn't budge.

Emma stuck her wooden clogged foot in the door and

tried her level best to pry it open a piece. Nothing doing. The man holding it was as strong as an ox.

"What do you want?" he said, sounding very short on patience.

Emma tried to shove against the door with her elbow. "Well, I'd like to speak to you," she said, trying as hard as she could to at least get a look at the deep baritone voice's face.

"Emma, run, run....." Jane shouted as soon as she found the breath to do so. Then she felt a hard hand clapped over her mouth and a riding crop poke into her guts.

"I know you've got my friend in there," the red-haired girl said accusingly. "You've got her there, and I'm going to call the police unless you let me in."

With that, Lucas Keating shoved the door shut and locked it hard. He turned to face his wife as the pounding on the door increased tenfold. The girl was shouting and pounding as loud as she could.

"Let me in there .... let me, or I'll call the hotel detective. I'll call the police. Let me in. Let me in."

Emma pounded and yelled into the door. A few passers-by in the hall stared oddly at her as they walked past. A couple of them hurried by to avoid looking at her.

"What the hell do we do now?" the man asked his wife.

She turned to the girl she had so firmly gripped by the mouth. "If you say one word, I'll horsewhip your friend to coleslaw. Do you understand?"

Jane nodded and let her jaw go slack. She had been fighting her blonde captor, but now she knew she must keep her head. She must keep her few remaining wits about her and think.

”We have to let her in,” Chloe said, tapping her riding crop hard against her leather-bound hip. ”Throw me my gown.”

Lucas Keating tossed his wife's black satin gown over to her, and she slipped it over her head as rapidly as she could as the pounding and the shouting continued unabated.

”Let me in, let me!” Emma let her fist fly into space as the door in front of them opened and admitted her to the dimly lit room.

”Come in,” the man said, bowing as though he were the last of the country's gentlemen. ”We've been expecting you.”

Emma doubted that very much. She felt her way uneasily into the vast hotel room. The thing was laid out like a ballroom of a plantation. And Rhett Butler was standing right in front of her. Then she saw a statuesque blonde in a long black gown advance toward her. She was definitely not Scarlett O'Hara.

”You've got Jane here, haven't you?” she said defiantly. She had to admit she felt a little strange, standing in that big room with the chandelier and the fireplace and these two rather well-dressed, handsome people standing before her. She also realized that she was terribly alone, that she hadn't called the police or the hotel detective, and that she had no idea what she was going to do when she did find out what they had done with her.

”Won't you sit down?” the man said, gesturing toward the scarlet red divan.

”I didn't come here to be sociable. Where is Jane?”

”Your friend is quite safe with us, I assure you,” the man said.

”I don't believe a word of it!” the enraged girl shouted, not knowing if it would be proper to knock over a lamp or a vase to prove her point.

"Arrrhhh," she heard coming from behind the door at the end of the room.

"She's in there, isn't she?" Emma said, standing up and racing toward the door.

Lucas dashed after her and made a flying tackle that brought her to the carpet.

She looked up to see the towering blonde bombshell standing over her.

"Your friend is in the bathroom," Chloe said, maintaining her cool and speaking in her haughtiest, high-born voice.

"Would you like to see her?" She snapped her fingers for her husband to let the girl free.

Emma stood up, a little shaken but none the worse for wear. "Yes." She felt terrified for some reason. Like cold chills were making an ice trail up and down her spine. She looked toward the door and heard the insane, muffled little cry come from behind it.

"Go on then, see her for yourself," the regal queen announced and pointed toward the bathroom.

The red-haired girl took a few tentative steps toward the door. She felt her heart growing heavier and beating faster in her chest. She felt fear rise like a vapor and cloud her reason. But she knew she must get to the door. She knew she must turn the hot, hard handle now in her hand. And she knew she must open it and look...

And right in front of her, sitting in an enormous executive-style swivel chair tied onto it like a side of beef was her best friend. And she had a gag in her mouth. Her eyes were wide and blinking. Her body had definite marks of a whipping or some kind of torture.

"Oh, my God!" the girl screamed as she rushed toward her. "What have they done to you, Jane?"

"Anrrn-hhhhhhhh," she replied, unable to speak with her mouth full.

"What have you done to her?" Emma said, turning in a rage toward her friend's assailants. "What have you done to my friend?"

"Shall we take that gag out of her mouth and find out?" the blonde witch replied casually. "You can ask her yourself if you like."

Emma had never seen such brazen behavior in her life. This woman was one cool cucumber, all right. The man seemed to do anything she wanted, though as powerfully built as he was, he could probably pulverize her in one blow.

She stood entranced as the woman snapped her fingers and pointed toward the bound and gagged bundle on the swivel chair.

Lucas Keating jumped at his mistress's command and ungagged the stretched-out slave.

Jane wiggled her mouth muscles around a little, trying to shake the numbness off.

"Jane," Emma said, falling to her knees in front of her, "what's going on here? What have these barbarians done to you?"

"Oh," Jane said, shaking her head back and forth, "they tied me up, bound me so hard I couldn't move, then they forced my head down on this man's cock."

"What?" Emma cried in bitter outrage. "How dare they!"

"And believe me when I tell you, Em," Jane said, finding her tongue again, "he has got one baseball bat of a prick pole on him.'"

"Oh, baby," Emma said, brushing the blonde tresses away that had fallen into her friend's eyes.

"They made me suck him, Em," the girl said, shaking her whole frame and feeling the tears well up in her eyes, "and this woman, she stuffed the wrong end of a bullwhip up my cunt and worked it up and down like a power switch."

"Holy Shit!" the red-haired girl wailed in sympathy. "That must have been terrible."

Jane choked back a few tears and the swelling that was working its way up in her throat, "I never said it was terrible, Emma." She stared into her friend's haunting amber eyes and blinked back a few more tears.

"It must have been, though, huh?" the friend said, full of sympathy.

"No," the blonde girl sobbed back, "I kinda liked it."

Emma felt her knees turn to applesauce as she felt the heavy iron grip of the man's hand on her shoulder. He pulled her up by the collar and whirled her around so that she came face to face with the blonde vixen, who now stood before her without her black gown, dressed in the meanest, blackest, most medieval-looking thing since the black castle of Falworth.

"You heard it from your friend's lips," the blonde wench bellowed. "Now, you will discover what it means to serve me."

Emma felt her whole body pitch forward and sprawl out onto the carpet. The man behind her must have given her the boot. Jane couldn't have done it. Not tied up the way she was.

"Try it, Em," Jane said from her swivel chair prison. "You might like it."

Emma had a pretty good idea that she wouldn't like it at all. This rough treatment was already getting to her. How could her friend possibly have fallen into the hands of these horror twins? She must have been drugged or hypnotized. She felt the carpet poke up rudely into her chin as the man's boot heel collared her neck and thrust it down hard onto the ground.

"Kiss your mistress's boot," the man ordered. From his surly, harsh tone, she knew he meant business.

Emma wormed along on her belly toward the waiting white witch. She brought her face toward the woman's boot, and it looked like she would kiss it. But she gathered all the saliva in her mouth and spat straight onto the shiny leather toe.

"Foul-mouthed little wretch!" the man shouted as he kicked her in the head.

Emma felt herself sprawling out and kicked into a somersault. She wound herself up like a hedgehog to avoid further blows to the head, but the man was beating her severely on the rear end. She felt a pair of hands rip her denim pants down over her hips, carrying her panties with them.

"Oww," she wailed as the flailing crop struck her on the butt.

"Now kiss my boot, Worm!" the woman said, scrambling

to her head and taking hold of a rough black leather bullwhip. "Kiss it and serve me the way I command, or I will beat you."

Emma felt herself grow rigid with fear and horror. These two could do anything, she knew, to prove their superiority. She trembled and quaked with fright as the rough, red places on her ass grew hot and throbbed with dead, white heat.

Jane sat in her chair, feeling totally ignored by the crowd. She wanted them to pay some attention to her. She wanted them to show her that they cared.

"Oh, Bob," she called out in a taunting, teasing tone, "I think you missed her ass. Better try again."

The man flew toward her with his whip raised over his head. He brought it down savagely on the tops of other alabaster white thighs.

She felt the whip sting her and saw into her throbbing flesh. The pain, the pure, unadulterated pleasure of the pain, made her cry out in agony and ecstasy, "Leave my friend alone," Emma cried out in fury. "Just lay off of her."

"Very well," the evil blonde queen spoke again, "we'll let her alone. But you will have to pay the consequences if we do."

"Oh, shit!" Emma said, pounding the carpet with her fist. Life seemed so very unfair to her just then.

She felt those rude, rough hands rip her plaid flannel shirt off her back and pull her bra off, though she tried to fight them. The two were just too much for her. And it was evident from the way they ripped those clothes off her they had experience with these things before. Much more than she had. All she had ever done was seduce senile landlords for the back rent.

"You will now suck your master's cock!" the harsh, punishing voice of the vile mistress poured out into her ear. "You will have no choice but to do as you are commanded."

"No," Emma cried, but the sting of the man's whip silenced her.

"Yes," the woman spat into her ear. Her voice was quiet now, quiet and deadly.

She heard the big man unzip his fly in a bold, agonizing stroke. Then she felt her hands yanked behind her back and her whole body pulled into a kneeling position. It must have been that blonde woman yanking her arms back there. She was as strong as an Amazon.

The rough carpet was rubbing hard against her knees as she felt her arms pulled further back into a position that made her breasts arch out hard in front of her.

She was only dimly aware of the big man's black fly thrust up in front of her face. "Suck my dick," he ordered, bringing his own whip handle down behind her head, forcing her down onto his enormous, heaving member.

She felt her lips meet his erect dick head. It was as hard as the wooden part of a golf club. And roughly the same size. She let her lips out to play on that smooth body surface. She had no other choice. The woman behind her was pulling her arms back so hard she feared they would be pulled right out of the sockets.

"God," she managed to scream before the rude cock stick silenced her words.

"Now, Filthy Street Whore," the blonde woman hissed at her, "you will discover the privilege of serving your master and your mistress. You will suck this man's cock until you can no longer draw a breath, until you slobber and wail and cry out in agony. And still, you will be forced to suck this man off."

Emma blinked as she looked up to see the man's massive shaft above the tip of his dick. The tip of his dick was being thrust right between her protesting lips. And behind him and a little to the right was the bitch queen. She was walking back and forth, back and forth, slapping her riding crop onto the palm of her hand and shouting her orders.

Okay, Emma thought as the cock log rammed its way down her pulsating raw throat. Who the hell is holding my arms? Then it hit her. Her darling roommate and bubbling, bouncing Bobsey Twin of a best friend. Jane Harris. Jane was holding onto her arms. The little bitch!

"Suck that cock, gutter bitch!" the man bellowed as he thrust the hot hard ramrod down her gulping mouth. "Suck it like I tell you."

Emma let the thick post plumb down her throat. It all but cut her air off as she gulped and gagged on it. That thing was so absolutely huge, so preposterously monstrously wicked. Plus, it was interesting. She had to confess that to herself. It was downright captivating.

Emma was aware of the blonde woman's stiff riding crop handle. She saw it poke through her master's outstretched legs and find its way to her quivering cunt hole. It poked and prodded at her as the man continued to shout and curse down to her face.

"Go on, my little slave," he ordered, "suck me and suck me

good. And then, when and if I've had my fill of you, I will ram this hot poker stick up your saintly white little ass."

Oh, no, Emma thought to herself hopelessly, not my ass. Not my poor battered, beleaguered little ass! These guys really show me no mercy, none whatsoever.

Jane gripped a tighter hold around her friend's wrists. She felt the hard, cruel welts on her backside cringe in pain with each move she made. She bowed her head as her master glared back at her with evil in his eyes. She felt thankful to be serving him. And she knew she would do whatever was asked of her. Whatever the man commanded, she would gladly do. Whatever the woman ordered, she would happily serve.

Two and a half years of rejection, debasement, and foul play. Two and a half years, longer really, of being in control of her life, and what had it gotten her? Nowhere. Nowhere at all, until now.

She looked over Emma's shoulder and smiled as the man sailed his rock-hard schlong in and down and around, out and around and down again back into her friend's gobbling hole. It looked so juicy and slimy and cocksure. So hard and eager and pulsating. She saw the veins stand out like highways on a roadmap. The sight made her ooze with juices. The sight of her master's grinding long schlong. It was beautiful. It was beautiful, and it was painful because she knew one thing. One thing is for sure. In order to protect her best friend from having her ass lacerated, she was going to have to volunteer to get fucked up the ass instead.

"Okay," Jane said, feeling the pain of the welts along her back sear into her subcutaneous layer. If they kept burning like that, they would burn into her brain. "Okay, I wish to reveal something to my captors."

"Worthless Wench!" Chloe spat, snapping the whip dangerously close to Jane's nose. "Did I give you permission to speak?"

"No, Great White Mistress, your Honor," Jane tried gamely to address the woman in a reverential tone, "but I want to say that I want to humble myself to you, all of you. I wish to serve you completely, you, two, and you, Emma... all of you, in fact."

"What is this ingrate talking about?" Lucas growled, pulling his thick meat out from Emma's mouth.

The conversation ceased briefly as the three women looked longingly at Bob's hot hard dick rod. It was so wet and juicy and dripping with the saliva and mucous from Emma's mouth. All three secretly wished the big brute would stick that honey log straight up their wazoos, but this wasn't the time or place for girlish fantasies.

"I wanna get rammed up the wrong way," Jane said, wishing the welts on her back would stop throbbing with pain long enough to unwrinkle her brow.

"What?" Emma cried. "You do?"

Emma couldn't help wondering if Jane, her old true blue friend, was trying to protect her. It was such a sweet thought. After holding her hands down and letting that man practically pulverize her with his hot, thick cock weapon, here she was offering to take it on the dark side, which might mean she wouldn't have to. What a pal!

"I am ready, great Mistress," Jane said, moving toward Chloe and casting her eyes toward the hotel carpet.

Chloe looked at her captor and snapped her fingers. Then she snapped her whip. "Down on your knees, lowly scum," the woman commanded.

By now, Jane knew she meant business. She slithered down to the carpet and felt Chloe's sharp boot heel dig into the flesh of her neck. Right now, that flesh was sore and bruised. It didn't hurt, or did it?"

Lucas maneuvered his dick around in his hands, keeping it hard and ready for whatever was to be found for him. He didn't really care which of these handmaidens he would plug, but he knew it had better be soon. Sticking his cock down that red-haired girl's throat had gotten him awfully hot under the collar.

"Kiss the fuck rug, Toots," Chloe shouted as she dug the heel of her boot even harder into Jane's neck. The feeling of power it gave her was delightful, delicious. And seeing her husband holding that hot, hard dick in his hand made her squirm under her leathers.

"You," Chloe commanded Emma, "hold the slave down so that she cannot move exactly as I bid you to do."

Emma walked over and got down on the rug. It was a little like a game but more serious, much more serious. "Yes, Mistress," she said, not wanting to take any chances getting that whip cracked against her fanny.

"That's better," Chloe seethed from between her teeth. "Get to work, now," she said, swiftly snapping her thick whip in Lucas's direction.

THE END

A Story from

Yesteryear's Stories Reflected Today
Yabot AB
www.yabot.se